Praise for

Under the Ashes

"Rankin's brisk-moving debut places a spirited heroine at the center of the 1906 San Francisco earthquake... Littlebeth's resilience and strong, memorable voice make this a vivid account of grace under fire."
—*Publishers Weekly*

"Debut author Rankin breathes life into the story of the 1906 San Francisco earthquake."—*Kirkus Reviews*

"Littlebeth's first-person narration, in vernacular prose, descriptively details settings and events and incorporates historical cultural references and vivid accounts of the devastating quake and its aftermath...fans of historical fiction will find plenty to like."—*Booklist*

"Littlebeth is feisty and never stops being her true self. An uplifting story where heart and smarts conquer prejudice and fear."—Sherry Shahan, author of *Skin and Bones*

"The calamitous and headstrong Littlebeth is one of my all-time favorite heroines. Readers will celebrate the courageous and heart-strong girl she becomes."—Sharon Lovejoy, author of *Running Out of Night*

Under the Ashes

Cindy Rankin

Albert Whitman & Company
Chicago, Illinois

To my daughter, Kate, who taught me it's okay
to be proud of yourself—CR

Library of Congress Cataloging-in-Publication Data

Names: Rankin, Cindy, author.
Title: Under the ashes / Cindy Rankin.
Description: Chicago, Illinois : Albert Whitman & Company, 2016.
Summary: In 1906, feisty eleven-year-old Elizabeth "Littlebeth" Morgan is shipped
off to live with her Aunt Sally in San Francisco with the hopes that she will be
tamed, but shortly after arriving the city is hit by a catastrophic
earthquake, forcing Littlebeth to fight for her survival.
Identifiers: LCCN 2016041531 | ISBN 978-0-8075-3637-7 (paperback)
Subjects: LCSH: San Francisco Earthquake and Fire, Calif., 1906—Juvenile fiction
CYAC: San Francisco Earthquake and Fire, Calif., 1906—Fiction. | Survival—
Fiction. | San Francisco (Calif.)—History—20th century—Fiction.
Classification: LCC PZ7.1.R37 Un 2016 | DDC [Fic]—dc23
LC record available at https://lccn.loc.gov/2016041531

Printed in the United States of America
10 9 8 7 6 5 4 3 2 1 LB 22 21 20 19 18

Cover illustration by Kyle Letendre
Cover design by Morgan Beck

For more information about Albert Whitman & Company,
visit our website at www.albertwhitman.com.

Chapter 1

Paso Robles, California
Sunday, April 8, 1906

Saved my little brother's life today. Turned out poorly for me, good for Joey, though. Hard truth is, being the bravest, quickest, most interesting girl in town puts me at a disadvantage. Ordinary folks—even my own family—can't seem to tolerate me.

Was on my best behavior when we came home from the Palm Sunday service. Had to be. There'd been trouble last week after I showed my class where the outlaw James brothers stayed here in the old days. My teacher said it was a reckless act of defiance and I was a bad influence. Mama, Papa, and especially Grandma were still vexed by what I'd done. I worked to redeem myself by doing extra chores and accepted my punishment of tending Joey, plus no dessert for two weeks, without complaint.

In the kitchen, Mama tied an apron over her church dress and then put the cast iron skillet on the stove.

"May I help?" I asked in a cheery tone.

"You up to something?" Mama saw me eyeing the apple pie Grandma had brought over. Sticky sweetness glistened around slits on top of the golden crust.

"No, ma'am," I said, turning away from temptation with a shrug. Couldn't keep my yearning from her.

Joey crawled under the kitchen table and spouted out his favorite song, "Jesus Loves Me," through spit bubbles. His main talents at two and a half years were constant drooling, nose dripping, and darting off whenever I reached for him. But this time I grabbed his leg and pulled him to me before he could escape.

"Aha!" I hoisted him into the air and twirled around. "You're caught, you slippery rascal."

We bumped into Mama as she put lard into the heated fry pan. It sizzled.

"Littlebeth Morgan!" Mama's nerves showed whenever I got near her burners because of the time I tried to scramble an egg and my pigtail caught fire. She took a breath then gently squeezed my shoulder. "You and

Joey play outside. That would be helpful."

"Yes, ma'am."

"Stay right by your brother. Don't take your eyes off him."

I understood the warning in her voice, meant to remind me of my solemn responsibility not to let him run off. "Yes, ma'am." Hoped she heard the earnestness in my reply.

Carrying Joey past the parlor, I walked slow enough to hear Grandma prattle on about my latest escapade. Papa cleared his throat now and then but didn't interrupt his mother's lecture. "She'll be twelve in October. She's untamed. Her shenanigans are an embarrassment."

Felt bad for Papa. Grandma could talk a blue streak about my faults. If that old bird had her way, I'd be in the house all day stitching samplers with verses describing the qualities of a well-bred young lady: silent, sweet, soft. Dull, duller, dullest.

Thank goodness she didn't live with us anymore. When Papa became the manager of Citizens Bank four years ago, he bought Grandma a cottage around the corner. But she always has Sunday dinner with us and comes over whenever she wants. Mama says that's to keep us on our toes, because Grandma once caught

Mama reading *McCall's* magazine instead of doing housework.

I put Joey down, and, as much for Grandma as for my little brother, I growled like a grizzly bear, spread my arms, and clomped after him. He squealed, pushed open the front screen door, and ran.

"You have to take the sass out of that lass," Grandma said to Papa, making sure those words followed me outside.

Joey zigzagged around the porch, then went down the steps to the yard on his bottom. Caught him halfway to the picket fence. Tickled him till he begged for mercy. Hummed in his ear while I held him tight and rolled us across the grass. His arms and legs relaxed inside my hug.

"Lil'bit, story, please, story." He couldn't say my whole name. Annoying, but sort of adorable.

I shook the quilt we'd used for a pretend picnic yesterday and forgot to put back in the house. Then I laid it underneath the oak tree and plopped down. Joey crawled onto my lap.

"A long time ago," I said, "the most wanted desperadoes in the whole Wild West, Frank and Jesse James, came to Paso Robles to hide from the law at their uncle Drury James's ranch."

Joey fell asleep before I got to the part when I took my classmates out to that old ranch site last week in Papa's wagon. Knew everything about those bank robbers from the dime novels I'd read. Figured telling some of their bandit deeds, in the very place they'd laid low, would show the class how exciting, and close, history could be.

Hoped they might finally appreciate me. Maybe even like me. It almost worked. Until Miss Hobson, the school board, and everyone's parents got so riled up about the outing. None of the kids will talk to me now. Their folks won't let them.

Eased myself out from under Joey, careful not to wake him. He was on his back so I made sure the oak's branches shaded his face while he napped. Mama said too much sun would give us freckles.

I circled the tree thinking about how wrong everything went last week. Then walked a little faster around the edge of the yard. The injustice of it all simmered my juices. Had to work off steam. Found my skipping rope near the house and started jumping. Counted 227 hops until my foot caught. I stumbled. "Drat, blast it!"

Feared my curses might rouse Joey. That he'd tattle on me. But he didn't stir; his baby snores held steady.

Decided to check Mama's garden for some ripe berries to soothe my mood. Looked over my shoulder at Joey as I went through the gate on the side of the house. He'd be in the land of nod a while longer. I'd only be gone a minute.

Didn't find ready fruit on the vines but pulled a few weeds for Mama. Coming back through the gate, I froze when I saw the dreadful triangle shape six paces ahead of me. It moved.

A rattlesnake was poking its big head out from under the house. The serpent flicked its tongue, shook its rattle.

Knew not to catch its eye. Prayed it would go back under the house. But it slithered into the yard. Its long body moved slowly in the warm sun. Problem was, the reptile separated me from Joey. I had no way to get to my brother. If the snake kept going in the same direction, it'd pass Joey by a wide space. Likely neither one would notice the other.

"Stay. Still." I said each word calmly, but my sleeping brother didn't hear. His arm flopped out to the edge of the quilt.

The rattlesnake stopped, lifted its head, and turned to eye Joey.

"Don't move. Please don't move," I whispered.

Just then, my little brother rolled onto his stomach. The snake shifted to face him, coiled itself, and rattled its warning again.

I needed a weapon. Needed one now. The rattler was still a fair distance from Joey, but if he moved again, the snake would see danger. It could attack. I looked around. Clenched my hands so tight my nails dug into my palms. Saw Mama's garden hoe leaning against the fence by the gate.

Joey curled the fingers of his right hand. A sure sign his thumb was about to go in his mouth. That motion would draw the snake. I grabbed the hoe. When Joey latched onto his thumb, the rattler straightened and slid fast toward my brother.

My legs burned as I raced behind the moving serpent. I straddled its tail and raised the hoe high overhead. Held my breath to true my aim then smote that critter to kingdom come.

Its severed head flipped onto the blanket, inches from Joey.

"Huzzah!" I yelled and let out a war whoop.

Saving Joey set my heart to pumping. How could my family stay mad at me now? Could almost taste the tender apples and flaky crust of Grandma's pie. Reckoned she'd give me a piece now and another after dinner.

Hardly heard my brother's screams or the *slam, bam, bam* of the screen door as Papa, Grandma, then Mama rushed down the steps. I was too busy imagining the shiny dime Papa might press into my hand and Mama's hug, sprinkled with tears of relief. There might even be a story in the newspaper about me being a vigilant sister on this holy day.

"Oh dear, oh dear," Mama cried.

"The head, keep away from the head!" Papa yelled.

Mama scooped my squealing brother off the blanket. "What have you done?" She looked at me then at the rattler's open mouth with fangs ready to bite.

I stood over the headless carcass, holding onto the hoe's handle, blade side up. My chest puffed out. "One whack," I said.

Papa snatched the hoe from me. His jaw tightened, his mustache twitched, but he said nothing. He used the tool to lift the snake, then held it out to balance the dangling body. It seemed to be jerking around trying to find its missing head.

Grandma spoke right up. "Littlebeth, you're a real Calamity Jane!"

What a dandy compliment. I'd read about the

adventures of Martha Jane Canary. My courage had earned Grandma's praise.

Then she went on.

"Look at you. Covered in dirt and snake guts, risking life and limb—yours and everyone around you."

How could she be so rude after I'd rescued her grandson from a terrible end? Why didn't she or anyone else say, *Well done, Littlebeth*?

Mama glanced at the open garden gate, then took Joey into the house, wiping snake blood from his cheek with her apron. Papa told me to get the shovel. "You're going to help me bury this thing so it can't cause any harm."

He walked the rattler, draped over the hoe, to the rubbish pit behind the house. Grandma followed, her arms stretched as far from her body as they would go, holding the four ends of the blanket together to carry the snake's head. "Something has to be done," she said to Papa's back.

I trailed behind them, dragging the shovel. There'd be no pie tonight.

* * *

We sat in the dining room picking at the meal Mama had prepared. She fretted about the food not being hot. Papa mumbled it was fine. Grandma stared at her plate.

Joey had most of his dinner smeared across his nose and cheeks. Mama gave him a piece of her roll then turned to me. "Why didn't you bring your brother inside when you saw the rattlesnake and tell Papa? That's what any other girl would have done."

"There wasn't time." I used my fork to bury peas under the mashed potatoes. Couldn't look at her. Might've had time if I hadn't gone into the garden.

Papa let out a deep humph, but I spoke up before he had a chance. "When the rattler saw Joey lift his thumb, it went after him lickety-split." Why couldn't Papa and Mama just thank me? "Lucky I'm so fast," I added.

Grandma sucked in too much air and coughed.

"That head landed next to your brother," Papa said. "Don't you know, even dead, the snake's venom could have poisoned Joey?"

Mama shuddered. "One touch of those fangs. One skin prick."

"Littlebeth," Papa said, "if you'd missed, that rattlesnake could have bitten the both of you." He wiped his napkin across his mouth and then tossed it on the table.

"But I didn't miss, Papa. And you're welcome."

"Young ladies don't talk back to their fathers." Grandma squinted at me. "My daughter would never—"

"Why get mad at what didn't happen?" I interrupted. "Can't you be happy Joey's alive?"

That's when Papa sent me upstairs to put my brother to bed.

I let Joey crawl up each step on his hands and knees while I listened to Grandma recite my cowgirl antics and derring-dos, until she said, "Your girl chased skunks into my house!"

"You know that was an accident, Grandma," I called from the top of the stairs. "And I helped you scrub out the stink."

"To bed, Littlebeth." Papa sounded tired.

"She races the boys," Grandma went on.

"And wins," I whispered to Joey, holding my hand over his mouth to keep the giggles in.

"…brags about her brains…"

"Tells the truth." I nuzzled Joey's neck.

"Not to mention taking your wagon to haul eight children into the wilderness on a school day without telling anyone what she was up to."

Had enough of Grandma. She'd never get over those skunks. Now she wanted Mama and Papa to be just as angry with me for teaching a history lesson Miss Hobson wouldn't allow. Before I took Joey to his room,

I heard Mama's loud sigh after Papa said how concerned he was about the school not wanting me back this term.

"And what she did today worries me," he said. "She has no fear."

Grandma said, "There's only one way to prevent her ruination."

I settled Joey down for the night. Then I prepared myself for a spanking by stuffing a folded sweater down my bloomers.

* * *

Papa didn't spank me. He barely spoke to me all week. Mama didn't say much either, but she stayed near when I did chores or played with Joey, always watching, even when I had my nose in a book. She offered to brush my hair at night, something she hadn't done in a long while. But the strangest thing was Grandma not coming over to complain about me for six full days. Couldn't figure out what had changed.

Chapter 2

Easter Sunday, April 15, 1906

Smelled bacon frying and heard voices downstairs. I kicked off the bedcovers and dashed to the kitchen. Everyone but Mama sat around the table.

"Happy Easter, sleepyhead." Papa held his coffee cup near his mouth.

Next to him, Grandma tilted the bread bowl toward me. "Sit. I made hot cross buns." She didn't say a word about my uncombed hair, bare feet, and unwashed face.

"Lil'bit, he came!" Joey pointed at our upturned Easter hats stuffed with straw and mounds of bright red, yellow, blue, and green eggs.

Spotted them first thing in front of our places. Was so relieved I hopped like the Easter Bunny himself. "He ate the carrot we left him too," I said, every bit as excited as my little brother.

It had been such a strange week that I feared those nests might be empty. Tossed about most of the night, worried Joey would be disappointed, and somehow I'd be to blame.

"You know," Mama said, standing by the stove, "he leaves those beautiful eggs to remind you of the Resurrection we celebrate today."

I turned to her. Mama's cheeks were pink from cooking. She handed me a plate. At the top, she'd laid two strips of bacon end to end, put the fried-egg eyes below them, and a wide smile of sliced strawberries across the bottom. Same Easter breakfast she made last year. Everything felt normal again. Took my seat beside Joey and started eating.

"Bunny's coming back to hide them," he said, wiggling and squirming in his chair.

Papa waved his fork at him, "Only if you get ready for church on time and behave during the sermon."

"Littlebeth," Mama said, sitting down, "I finished your new Easter dress last night."

Joey kicked me. "What happens after church?" he asked.

"Then," I said, crunching bacon, "we'll search the

yard, and if we find every egg, the bunny leaves us chocolates under our dinner napkins." I swallowed, thinking about the taste of candy. "Papa, it's been two weeks. May I have dessert again, please?"

"Yes, but…" He took a sip of coffee then said, "Littlebeth, we've made a decision."

I'd just put half a bun in my mouth. Couldn't ask what he meant until I chewed it down. Papa shook his head at my fat cheeks and clicking jaw. "Tomorrow, you're going to take the train to San Francisco," he said.

"By *mythelf*?" Crumbs fell out with the words. I'd never ridden on a train before. The idea of a new adventure filled my mind and didn't leave room to wonder why I'd been given this Easter gift—better than chocolate or hot cross buns. Maybe they'd decided to thank me for saving Joey after all. I stood to hug Papa.

He motioned me down and dropped in the particulars. "You'll need to attend a new school for the rest of the year and stay with your Aunt Sally."

Everything soured. I remembered my aunt's pinched nose and twitchy lips, too thin to hold a smile. She had Grandma's sharp cheekbones, but I couldn't recall if she also had her mother's razor tongue. Don't think Aunt Sally said more than "please," "thank you," and "Do children always make so much noise?" when she visited us last Christmas.

Grandma beamed. "The Presbyterian Academy for Girls, and my Sally will turn you into a proper, refined young lady."

* * *

On our walk to Easter service, Mama held my hand. Before we entered the church, she adjusted my bonnet and pulled out a piece of straw.

I'd been silent since we left the house. The plan for my salvation cut deep. I had to be sent away, had to stop being me.

Reverend Douglas asked the congregation to pray for my safe journey. From the pews behind us, I felt a breeze of happy sighs at the news of my departure.

Chapter 3

Monday, April 16, 1906

A block from the train depot, I scuffed the toes of my black patent Easter shoes into the dirt of Pine Street so I could take a layer of home with me to San Francisco.

From six paces ahead, Grandma turned and saw me do it. "Littlebeth!" She squeezed my name out through tight-pressed lips.

Hated the way she said it. Made me sound like a baby even though I'm the tallest eleven-year-old in town. Knew Grandma didn't want her Sally thinking they'd send me off with dirty shoes. I smiled at her. She tapped her foot.

Mama yanked my hand. "Don't dawdle."

Grandma carried a small basket like a purse, the

handle slung over the crook of her arm, held tight against her ribs. "No tomfoolery. Understand?" She shook a bony finger in my direction then gripped my hand, the one Mama wasn't already holding, and pulled like a plow horse stung by a bee.

Papa and Joey had left before us in the wagon to haul the trunk—an old wooden one I'd found in Mama and Papa's bedroom after church yesterday, already half packed. Mama must have spent days getting my clothes ready for this trip without me knowing a thing about it.

By the time we reached the station, Grandma huffed from walking so fast. The locomotive belched steam— probably from the strain of standing still. Papa waited on the platform next to a passenger carriage. He gestured for us to join him. Joey was sprawled over Papa's shoes, fiddling with the spats.

"Thought you wouldn't make it," Papa said.

Except for his ginger-colored hair, he didn't resemble his mother or sister. He was large, strong, and kind-hearted, and I couldn't believe he'd let Grandma talk him into this.

I'd lain awake last night hatching ways to change Papa's mind, but he had it set. Stubbornness was one thing he had in common with his mother.

Folks scurried about with parcels and satchels and hugs good-bye. My entire family surrounded me—to prevent my escape. A shrill whistle blew. Joey covered his ears. "I wanna go home," he whined in a pitch higher than the whistle.

I bent over, picked him up. Wanted one of his soft hugs and slimy kisses. He twisted in my arms and reached for Mama. I held on.

Grandma shoved her basket at me. "For you to eat on the train."

Joey made a grab for it. Mama took him from me and smoothed his hair.

I clutched the basket handle as daintily as possible with my hands balled into fists. Had on Mama's white gloves, which were too big for me, but she insisted I needed them for the city. Bulges beneath a red-checked napkin in the basket called for my attention. I lifted the cloth and sniffed. Ah, buttermilk biscuits filled with apricot preserves and slivers of ham.

Grandma was a mean old devil, but she baked like an angel. Her lemon-butter cakes, sugar cookies, and pies always took blue ribbons at the county fair.

I smiled, showing my manners. "Thank you."

"Don't be a glutton," she said. "Make it last."

"Not polite to call someone names, Grandma. Especially someone you're saying good-bye to." I pushed the brim of my hat back to level a stern gaze, but the overlong fingers of Mama's gloves flopped into my eyes, making me blink like a nervous Nellie.

Joey giggled. "Do it again, Lil'bit. Do it again."

Mama hushed him. "You need a haircut, young man," she said. He laid his head on her shoulder. "We'll stop at the barbershop on the way home."

She started to say something to me, but Grandma beat her to it. "You'll soon discover that a young lady has to learn her place."

I held on to *discover*, tried to ignore the rest. San Francisco, a grand city by the sea, awaited. Aunt Sally couldn't corral me for long. I'd *discover* new things there and have adventures in spite of their plans for me.

That whistle tooted again. Joey let out another howl. I crossed my eyes and stuck out my tongue to make him laugh. He waved, ready for me to leave. Ready for the sarsaparilla he'd have later as a treat—after his haircut, after I'd gone.

Something caught in my throat made me swallow hard.

Grandma glanced at Mama, then at me, and said,

"Sally will tame your bumptious ways. High time some-one did."

In that instant, I realized Grandma blamed Mama for my antics. That irritated me more than anything, and, blast it, I was plenty perturbed.

"Mama, thank you for sewing this beautiful dress," I said, my words as thick as honey. I brushed a gloved hand over the gingham skirt and stared at Grandma.

"Try to keep it clean," Mama said.

"Littlebeth, when you're in the city, mind your p's and q's." Papa used his no-nonsense voice. "We may live in a small town, but we are *not* country hicks."

I stiffened my posture. "Yes, sir."

"Don't lose this." He stuck my ticket inside the bas-ket. "Keep your fanny glued to your seat until you ar-rive in San Francisco. Sally will be there to meet you."

Mama drew near and whispered, "Your aunt might need to get used to having you around, so, please, walk and talk softly."

The rosewater Mama dabbed behind her ears made me want to lean against her and breathe in deep, but I stepped back. Had to get used to being on my own. "Yes, ma'am."

"All aboard!" called the conductor.

My heart skittered. Grandma patted my back. Mama hugged me. Joey rubbed his wet nose on my cheek.

Papa held my elbow as I climbed the steps to the train. "Promise me you'll behave." His anxious tone made me queasy. I almost dropped the basket. Tightening my hold, I nodded.

Mama stood next to Papa and said, barely loud enough for me to hear, "I'm afraid we're tossing her out of the frying pan and into the—"

"Now, now," I heard Papa say before I went into the car. "It's Sally we should worry about."

The conductor sat me by the window. My family waved. Only Mama looked sad. I pulled her gloves off, folded them neatly, and put them on the checkered napkin covering Grandma's biscuits. Picked up a newspaper on the empty seat next to me and opened it wide to cover my face. Didn't want them to see the tear slipping out of my eye. Didn't want them to think I'd miss them. I concentrated on the story about a speech the president gave:

President Roosevelt criticized the muckrakers who write too much about the misdeeds of business and the government's weak laws.

He admitted there were politicians who betray the public trust who must be exposed, and corrupt businessmen who must be prosecuted. He said, "The men with the muckrakes are often indispensable, but only if they know when to stop raking muck."

Held the pages tight, determined not to look at the people sending me away. Bully-Boy Teddy, as Papa calls our president for always saying *bully* when he likes something, had a point. There comes a time when enough muck has been raked. You have to get on with other things. Grandma said I had to learn my place. She meant there was no place for me here. The train's whistle sounded. We chugged forward. I let go of the paper so I could wave to Joey, but he wasn't there.

None of them were.

Chapter 4

The train click-clacked along the tracks. We passed the granary, the mercantile, an empty lot, a livery, and then oak trees, one after another. Spanish missionaries called this place El Paso de Robles—the Pass of Oaks—because there are so many of them here. I tried to memorize everything outside the window, afraid I'd forget once I got buttoned into the city. The train's rocking motion comforted me as I watched our rounded hills pass by, their green coats already fading in the spring sun. Soon they'd turn to summer gold and look like sleeping lions. I'd miss that.

"This seat taken, little girl?"

I looked up to see a lady about Mama's age. She wore

a purple knitted hat and a tan coat. Shaking my head no, I moved the crumpled newspaper to make room for her.

"You're a brave girl to travel on your own. How far are you going?" Her perfume was spicier than Mama's floral scent, but I liked it almost as much and was happy for the company.

"I've upset my family so they're...um...exiling me the way the French did to Napoleon. But instead of Elba—that's an island off Italy's west coast—my family's sending me to school in San Francisco and making me live with my aunt."

"Goodness, how did a smart girl like you upset them?"

The lady had a gentle smile. Seemed sensible too. I shifted in the seat and leaned back against the window to study her.

"Get on in Paso Robles?" I asked. Didn't recognize her, but I wasn't going to tell my problems to someone who might know Grandma, Papa, or Mama.

"I boarded in San Luis Obispo," she said then dipped her chin toward the front of the carriage. "I was in the car ahead, but a pesky boy kept kicking the back of my seat. I had to find a new place to sit or lose my temper."

The idea of exploring perked up my spirits. Before

I could ask how old the boy was, she said, "Glad to find a nice girl to pass the time with. Mind if I knit while we chat?" She pulled open a tapestry bag and took out knitting needles, caramel-colored yarn, and what looked like a doll's blanket.

"I'm trying to finish a sweater for my son in San Jose," she said.

That sweater was a long way from done or her son was a circus midget.

"How many children does your aunt have?" she asked while preparing her needles.

"None. She's not married."

"Oh?" She positioned the yarn in her lap.

Told the lady what I knew about Aunt Sally. "She's five years younger than Papa. Went to school in San Francisco, and she has a shop, but I don't remember what kind."

"How fortunate and unusual to have a business of her own, whatever it may be."

Had a feeling she wanted to hear more about my aunt, but there was nothing more to say. I watched her click those knitting needles together so fast they moved in a blur. Settled into my seat and thought about eating one of Grandma's biscuits.

"So tell me how you upset your family." She glanced over and then focused on her work.

"Well," I said, my eyes on her hands, "the skunks started it, Frank and Jesse James made it worse, and a rattler finished me off."

The lady's eyebrows arched, but she kept tapping and twisting those needles.

"I wanted to help my grandma," I said, pausing to let that sink in. "So I tried to shoo a skunk and her two babies out of Grandma's yard. But she'd left her backdoor open for the evening breeze, and those skunks ended up in the middle of her quilting circle. Sprayed everyone's handiwork and most of the house."

"Oh my." The lady wrinkled her nose. Her nimble fingers moved the needles over and under, again and again. "A good deed gone awry," she said.

"Exactly." I liked her. But thinking about Grandma rumbled my tummy.

"Hungry?"

"I guess." Didn't want to admit the noise was anger, not emptiness.

"Reach into my bag," the lady said. "There's a sandwich wrapped in paper. Take half, leave the rest for me."

Biting into soft bread and cheddar cheese calmed

me. "Thank you," I said. Bits of cheese fell from my lips. The nice lady didn't correct me for talking with my mouth full. I nudged Grandma's basket against the wall with my foot. Might share that later.

The lady tugged a snag from the yarn, adjusted her needles, and knitted away. "What about Jesse James?" she asked.

I told her how Miss Hobson wouldn't let me give a report on the outlaws so I'd taken matters into my own hands for the sake of my classmates. Left out the part about using Papa's wagon without permission and being truant, but left in how we got home after supper-time, and all the grown-ups were waiting at my house. Hopping mad.

"You scared them," the lady said, while using her needles to push, loop, and pull yarn into rows.

Hadn't she understood? They were angry. Not afraid.

The conductor walked up the aisle. "Salinas, next stop, Salinas." He bellowed the words in a singsong way then went on to the next carriage.

"Excuse me, please." I stood and shuffled by her.

"What about the rest of your story?" she asked.

"Need to stretch my legs. I'll be back soon."

"Don't get lost now," she said.

I wondered about her. "Ma'am, it's a train. No one could lose their way."

Heading to the forward car, I teetered as the train swayed over the tracks. Had to hold on to the seat backs. Walking felt just like a fun-house ride. I bumped into a sleeping man's head.

"Hey," he grumbled.

"Sorry."

I knocked a woman's large, feathered hat over her brow.

"Watch it."

"Sorry."

I looked back to see the knitter's eyes on me. I smiled and opened the door. A whoosh of air came in. Closed it quickly behind me. Nearly bumped into a boy smoking a cigarette.

He leaned against a metal gate bordering the outside walkway between carriages. Wind swirled his brown hair. The wide part of his knickerbockers flapped.

"Hold on," he said. "It's rocky out here over the coupling." His cigarette flared between his lips.

I held on to my hat with one hand and wedged myself next to him against the gate.

"We could be lookouts for train robbers," I said.

He laughed then asked if I was getting off in Salinas.

"No. You?"

"Uh-huh." He offered me his smoke. "Want a puff?"

"I'm only eleven."

"Yeah? I'm twelve."

Reckoned if I turned him down, he'd stop talking to me. Didn't want that. "Okay."

He handed it to me. Our fingers brushed. I raised the cigarette almost to my lips and flicked the ash like I'd seen Papa do a thousand times. Cinders blew back on my skirt. I brushed them away.

"Go on." The boy grinned.

"You look kind of like Jesse James," I said.

"Yeah?"

"I know all about him. His middle name was Woodson. His uncle had a ranch near my town. Jesse visited him there. He had to take a steamship from New York to Panama then he crossed the isthmus. I'd like to do that, wouldn't you? He took another steamer to San Francisco and—"

"Give it back if you're only gonna hold it and gab." He reached for his cigarette.

I took a quick puff and coughed.

The conductor opened the forward door. He stepped out. "What are you two doing?"

I dropped the cigarette. The conductor looked at it.

"That girl took my smoke," the boy said. His eyes gleamed like Mr. Edison's electric lights. The rat.

But then he said, "She told me I was too young for cigarettes."

Oh golly. First time anyone had lied, or even tried, to get *me* out of trouble.

"She's right," the conductor said. "Now back to your seat, little lady." He pulled open the door to my car.

I grabbed the boy's hand and shook it. "Littlebeth Morgan from Paso Robles," I said. "On my way to San Francisco."

"Tom," he said.

The conductor escorted me to my seat beside the knitter.

"Get lost?" She smiled.

I shrugged, then pressed my nose against the window as we pulled into the station. When we stopped, Tom jumped off the train and hurried over to a waiting man and woman. He turned to look at my carriage. I waved. He didn't see me or didn't want to wave back. Never had any luck making friends.

New passengers boarded and settled in. We moved on. The knitter rested her hands for a minute. "Where'd you leave off? Oh yes, everyone was mad."

I stared out the window a few seconds longer, cleared my throat, and began explaining. "Miss Hobson hated how smart I was. She told Mama and Papa the other students suffered because of it. I tried not to answer so many questions in class or to correct her poor spelling or miscalculations—the woman doesn't understand fractions. Or geography. She didn't know our Salinas River flows north like the Nile in Africa. Not interested in history either. After the outing to the old James ranch, she didn't want me back in her class."

The knitter stopped and looked at me.

"But she's going to miss my help, and the class will too."

Pointing to her bag with one needle, the lady said, "I'm feeling peckish. Please give me the rest of my sandwich."

I handed it to her. She unwrapped the paper, spread it over her lap, and took a very big, unladylike bite. That sandwich vanished in two more chomps. I grinned at her. Maybe all ladies didn't have to be properly refined. Gave me hope.

"That's why you're on your way to a new school." She picked up her needles again and went back to work.

The conductor walked through, checking tickets. As he passed us, the knitter asked him, "How long until San Jose?"

"Few more hours, madam. How's the little lady? Behaving herself?"

"She's a real talker." Neither one of them looked at me.

After several minutes, the lady said, "You mentioned a rattlesnake."

I showed her how it had ogled Joey. Imitated its tongue and slither. She winced as she knitted. When I acted out chopping off its head, her jaw dropped, making a noise like her tongue had stuck to the roof of her mouth.

"That's why I've been exiled to San Francisco." I reached down for the basket. Wanted to give her one of Grandma's biscuits.

"You scared them," she told me for the second time.

Changed my mind about sharing and turned toward her. "But I *didn't* miss!" Why couldn't anyone understand that?

"Sounds like your folks want to keep you safe and help you become a fine young woman by giving you the best education they can."

Grown-ups have a habit of siding with other grown-ups. I lifted my spine, sat back, and stared straight ahead. Using my most mature voice, I said, "Well, I suppose if you don't like who a person is or what they do, you send them away and hope they turn into somebody else."

The lady nodded, paying more attention to her needles than me. She knitted so furiously I don't think she heard me say, "When Napoleon went back to France, he hadn't changed at all."

Vowed I wouldn't change either. Didn't matter what my family or anyone else thought of me. Great people were rarely appreciated in their own time. I'd show them all how wrong they were not to want me around. Didn't need them anyway.

I closed my eyes and contemplated my destiny. Imagined how I'd travel the world as a journalist or an explorer or both, writing about my thrilling exploits and lecturing at the finest universities. Someday there'd be parades in my honor—banners flying, drums pounding, and crowds cheering.

By the time we were rolling into San Jose, I'd eaten half of Grandma's biscuits. I offered the lady one after she tied the last knot on the sweater. Couldn't believe she'd finished it, although the length of the sleeves didn't match.

She bit into the buttermilk biscuit. "Oh my, that's good." Folding her son's gift into the knitting bag, she said, "I enjoyed our chat."

A dab of apricot jam stuck to her upper lip and moved when she talked.

"Make your folks proud." She stood to leave.

"Have a nice visit," I said. "Hope your son likes the sweater even if it isn't perfect."

Chapter 5

My face had been pressed against the window ever since we left San Jose. A small line of drool ran from the corner of my mouth down my chin. Must have dozed off counting barns and windmills—ten times more up here than back home. The hills were greener, dotted with different kinds of trees, more than our oaks, and more houses too. I felt a hand on my arm, rubbed my eyes, and turned to face the conductor. He smiled then moved slowly through the car, singing, "San Francisco, last stop, San Francisco."

As we neared the city, buildings multiplied, grew taller, and were squeezed tighter together. When we pulled into the station, I caught sight of Aunt Sally on the platform. She held the top of her wide-brimmed black hat with one hand while waving a handkerchief with the other. The locomotive screeched to a stop, snorting the last gasps of steam after its long journey.

I took my time getting presentable, straightened my dress and straw hat, put Mama's gloves back on, and picked up the basket. On my way out, I searched the empty carriage for anything interesting left behind. Found a dime on the floor and two nickels on a seat cushion next to a flier for Frank's Freshest Fish on the Wharf. It had a drawing of a man in an apron holding a fish by the tail. The fish says to the man, "I prefer to be stewed."

The conductor came through the car just as I slipped the last nickel inside Mama's glove and shoved the flier into my basket. "Someone here to meet you, little lady?"

"Yes, sir. My aunt. That's her with the hankie. Golly, she's as skinny as a matchstick and just as red-faced."

The conductor cleared his throat. Must get sore with all that yelling he does to get passengers on board and warbling the names of stops along the way.

He followed me down the steps and herded me over to Aunt Sally. "Ma'am, I believe this is your niece. Good luck to you both." He touched the bill of his cap before walking away.

Aunt Sally's flushed face looked exactly like Joey's did the time he bit into a persimmon expecting something sweet. Bitter disappointment.

"I assume you brought more than that basket for your stay, Elizabeth."

No one ever called me that. She was already trying to turn me into someone else. She dabbed the tip of her hankie on her tongue and started rubbing that spit-soaked cloth across my mouth, digging into the corners, then swiping my chin a couple of times. Wanted to swat her with the basket, but I feared losing the last of those biscuits.

"You are a sight, child. Jam and crumbs all over you."

Failed the first test of my refinement by not arriving with a clean face.

"Now, do you have a clothing case or not?" she asked.

I grumbled a yes. She marched me over to the baggage car where several men were unloading large valises and leather-covered trunks with curved tops and brass studs. Aunt Sally had me point out Papa's old wooden box with his name stenciled on the flat top: Morgan, John. I'd told Joey it looked like an Army trunk and said Papa had probably been one of Teddy Roosevelt's Rough Riders, charging up San Juan Hill in Cuba.

Mama shook her head at that. Grandma said *poppycock*, her favorite word for my imagination.

A padlock dangled from the trunk's latch. I wondered how many places this scuffed box had been. Maybe not Cuba, but I hoped somewhere interesting for Papa's sake. Would have to find out the next time I saw him, whenever that might be. Was too mad to ask before I left.

Mama had put the trunk key inside one of the gloves so I wouldn't lose it. I shook my hands to make sure it was still there and smiled at the sound of it clinking into the coins I'd collected.

Thought of Grandma's biscuits and how I'd saved the rest of those delicious tidbits for Aunt Sally so she could taste her mother's home cooking again. Standing next to her, though, I decided to hold off telling her about them. She didn't look like a woman who ate very much, and I might get hungry later. Besides, she was busy giving one of the men her address and a dollar to deliver the trunk.

My aunt, the refined lady, had not yet said hello to me or asked how the train ride had been or if I needed to use the privy, which I did. Before I could mention it, she took me to the telegraph office inside the depot to send a message, letting Mama and Papa know I showed up.

After that, Aunt Sally grabbed my hand and hurried me outside and down a wide boulevard to the cable car stop. I forgot about peeing—Grandma calls it *making water*, Mama says *freshen up*, Papa pretends he's *draining the pipes*, and Joey usually announces, *Oops, I had an accident*, but I like to call it what it is, even though that may be one of the reasons I ended up here with Aunt Sally.

Every thought evaporated after only a few steps into San Francisco. My mouth gaped in wonderment. Oh, I swear pictures on postcards and in magazines and books can't compare with the sight of a real bustling, hurly-burly city. Colors, movement, and sounds from every direction, and smells I'd never smelled before. Jumbles of folks hurried here and there, up and down sidewalks. And when they crossed a street, the dashing they had to do between all the wagons and carriages— horseless ones too—made me gasp for their safety. Busiest place I'd ever seen. My head swiveled back and forth to take in giant signs and buildings with rooftops almost as high as the sky. Tried to see everything at once. My poor brain felt like a marble spinning round and round inside my skull.

"Stop gawking. You're dragging your feet." Aunt

Sally tugged my arm, pulling me toward a waiting cable car. "We must get home before your trunk arrives."

I'd seen drawings of cable cars, but they couldn't compare to this big, shiny, real one with its open sides. We climbed the steps. A man took Aunt Sally's coins, then swung the chain of a polished brass bell to sound three clangs. We plunked ourselves onto a wooden bench that faced the street. Off we went.

"Hold on," Aunt Sally said. "People have fallen out on some of these hills."

Now that would be something to see! The car moved up the street, then continued up, up. That hill rose so high, it seemed like a small mountain. Wondered if my aunt had ever taken a tumble. Just then the cable car's nose pointed straight down as if we were going off the edge of a cliff. My stomach jumped, and my need to pee returned. Aunt Sally flung a stiff arm in front of me as a brace. I silently blessed her.

Just as startling as that steep angle down was how slowly we descended it. I expected to be hurtling through the air, crashing into the five-story building on the corner at the bottom. Cable cars must have powerful brakes, or there wouldn't be so many people walking around alive in San Francisco.

Four stops and one turn later, Aunt Sally said, "This is it." She pulled me off the bench, which took a fair amount of strength, because I'd gripped the edge so hard my fingers stuck to the seat.

"Move along," she said. "Fog's coming in." Her hand clutched mine until my knuckles cracked.

Sometimes we had winter fog in Paso Robles. The thick, cover-everything kind. It was there from the time you woke up until you went to bed, unless it was a spring fog that disappeared with the afternoon sun. But I'd never seen anything like the flowing gray ribbons of mist that chased us now. They moved swiftly, weaving themselves into a gossamer cloak.

"How far to your house?" I wiggled my hand free and shifted the basket between us.

"Two and a half blocks. It's an apartment, Elizabeth, above my shop. Not a house. This is the city." Her voice had the same tone Grandma used to explain why a girl my age shouldn't run like a tomboy and sweat like a horse.

How long would it take Aunt Sally to refine me? Without a privy soon, I'd fail more than the clean-face test.

Chapter 6

We rushed across the street. Had to stop short for a covered buggy whizzing by—mindful, even in our haste, of where we placed our feet to avoid horse droppings. Muck, as President Roosevelt called it when he talked about the muckrakers. Wondered if Aunt Sally liked Bully-Boy Teddy as much as Papa did. Before I could ask, she pulled me along and pointed at the large two-story brick building ahead of us. It took up half the block. A few steps from the curb, a team of draft horses pulling a wagon broke through the misty fog. We jumped onto the sidewalk to avoid being run over and saw bold, black lettering on the side panel: Southern Pacific Railroad. The wagon slowed.

"We barely made it before your trunk." Aunt Sally paused to catch her breath. "I must commend Mr. Harriman for the efficiency of his railroad enterprise," she said.

She reached into her purse, pulled out the hankie she'd used to clean my face, and fluttered it over her head to signal the deliverymen in the wagon. "Here we are—over here, sirs!"

The wagon's driver waved. He turned his team around, moved the horses alongside us, then set his brake. His partner climbed over the bench seat into the back and dropped the rear hatch.

The driver jumped to the sidewalk and handed my aunt a piece of paper to sign. While they talked, I looked at the building that would be my new home. There were several ground-level shops. The window of the nearest one had curlicue white letters painted across the top of the plate glass:

Miss Sally Morgan's
Fine European Lace and Linens

An open-weave curtain covered the bottom half of the window. You could look right through its patterned holes to see folded tablecloths, handkerchiefs, lace collars, and veils displayed on the wide shelf below. Did this frill and fluff add up to refinement? I reckoned I had a long apprenticeship ahead, because all I could think about was how the curtain reminded me of Papa's fishing net.

Closing my eyes, I wished it were last summer when my family camped out in the mountains near a flowing creek. I used Papa's net to scoop up the wiggling steelhead trout he'd hooked on his line. Mama fried it for dinner in an old skillet over the campfire. Nothing had ever tasted so good or warmed my insides so completely.

"Do you have a cinder in your eye?" Aunt Sally's voice pulled me back to the city.

Blinking to keep a tear from spilling, I said, "No, ma'am. Suppose I'm tired. And hungry." I didn't tell her I was longing for the time when my family liked and wanted me. Instead, I pulled the flier out of my basket. "Have you heard of Frank's Freshest Fish by the Wharf? Maybe we could go there and buy a—"

"You'll wear me out if you don't learn restraint, child." Aunt Sally held a key with her thumb and finger, the way a lady holds the handle of a teacup, and told the deliverymen, "The trunk goes up there." She gestured toward a staircase nestled in an alcove of the building between her storefront and a haberdashery on the other side.

At the rear of the wagon, the men discussed who would take the lead on the stairs while my aunt hurried up to unlock her door.

"Do you have a water closet?" I called behind her. "I've an urgent need."

"Respectable ladies don't discuss needs." She waved me up and said, "Regard your manners in public. Restraint, restraint!"

How many more *re* words would I have to suffer? *Regret* came to mind. On the eighth step, I determined that my family and Aunt Sally would become acquainted with regret before I ever became refined or restrained.

The stairs ended at a landing abutted by a brick wall. Identical wooden doors faced each other across the landing. Aunt Sally turned to the left, inserted her key, and opened the door. "Inside, through the kitchen, on the right is the necessary room."

"Does the hat-shop owner live there?" I pointed at the other door.

"Yes, yes." She fumbled, dropped the key, then squatted to retrieve it.

Behind her, I bounced from one foot to the other, waiting for her to clear the way. The need I couldn't mention grew ever more urgent.

Heavy footfalls on the steps startled Aunt Sally. She lost her grip on the key. Dropped it again. Her bent knees gave way, putting her flat on her fanny.

"My trunk!" I turned to meet it. The cold clasp of my aunt's hand around my ankle made me squeak like a trapped mouse. The shock of it sent me tumbling into the arms of the gentleman walking out of the door across from hers. The man wore a black suit and a bowler.

"Careful. That's a long way down." He steadied me on the landing, then looked at my aunt struggling to get up. Her face was as red as it'd been at the depot.

"Oh my, my, Miss Morgan. Let me help you." The gentleman put his hands under Aunt Sally's arms to lift her.

I swear she almost sparked and caught fire. Her face was that crimson, her voice that crackly.

"Mr. Steinberg, stop. I can manage."

"Clear the way, folks. Coming through." The driver huffed his words fast. He was about to crest the top step, holding the bottom edge of my trunk behind him. His partner, who bore most of the weight several steps below, groaned.

Mr. Steinberg swooped Aunt Sally off the ground and carried her into the apartment. I scrambled in on his heels, taking off Mama's gloves so I could help. But first I placed them ladylike on the parlor settee, careful not to spill my coins or key. The deliverymen followed me inside. With my aunt still in his arms, Mr. Steinberg quickly looked around. He chose a nearby armchair and settled her onto its cushions.

"Where do you want this?" the wagon driver asked.

Aunt Sally turned her nose to a closed door off the parlor. Seemed like she'd lost the power of speech.

I opened the door for the men. Curiosity made me follow the trunk, even though my unmentionable need fought for attention. Ahead, I stared at the large bed with a fancy, carved mahogany headboard. Three emerald-green, tufted pillows adorned the white crocheted coverlet. A bed for a princess! Against one wall sat a mahogany chest of drawers and a dressing table with a padded bench; on the opposite side of the room was a matching wardrobe. Of course, there were lace curtains on the window.

My aunt had put me in the finest bedroom I'd ever seen. She rose considerably in my esteem until I knocked into a plain, canvas cot set up just inside the door. A colorless pillow, folded sheets, and a brown wool blanket were neatly stacked on it.

The deliverymen dropped the trunk and left. Any flicker of hope fizzled. No happy ending to my exile.

That royal bed seemed to smirk at me. Wanted to rip it apart and throw a full-blown tantrum like some runny-nosed kid. Like my brother. But Joey would never have been sent away. Restrained into refinement. Forced to sleep on a plain cot. No, he was home with Mama's cooing and Papa's tickles. I dropped my hat and Grandma's basket on the cot.

Had to find the privy before everything inside me drained out. I rushed through the parlor. Heard Aunt Sally stammer, "Mr. Steinberg, this really isn't appropriate."

Expecting the man to be doing something dastardly, I turned, only to see him holding a glass of water to Aunt Sally's pursed lips. I bumped into the round dining table. A blue vase filled with yellow daffodils wobbled but stayed upright. An archway led to the small kitchen and, next to it, the necessary room.

When I returned to the parlor, Mr. Steinberg was holding his hat over his heart. "I am always ready, Miss Morgan, to assist you in any way you'll allow."

She was on her feet. "Rest assured, I'm fine. My niece, a

country girl, simply knocked me down in her exuberance."

My jaw dropped at her lie, but a knot choked off the words I wanted to say. Had restraint already gripped me? Or maybe I was too weak from hunger to speak.

Mr. Steinberg left. Aunt Sally closed the door behind him then slumped back into her chair. Teardrops, big as any I'd ever seen, burst from her eyes and kept gushing.

She must have hurt herself when she fell outside the door, because those sobs were so strong that her whole face changed. Her lips puffed up to twice their normal size, while her eyes squinted and shrank from all that flowing water. Her nose darkened to a purplish bruise, and her chin shook something fierce. She wailed like a banshee. Though I'd never heard a banshee's cry, I'd read plenty of Irish folktales that perfectly described the terrible sound.

Pain is ugly. Aunt Sally was in awful pain.

I went for the basket, took off the checked napkin, pulled out one of Grandma's biscuits, and returned to the parlor. Kneeling beside my miserable aunt, I offered her the napkin.

"Wipe your nose with this, Aunt Sally. It smells like your mother." I stroked her arm the way Mama soothes me when I cry. It seemed to ease her.

"You need something good to eat." I handed her the biscuit. "Grandma made this."

She breathed deep, rattled breaths and sighed before fingering the little sandwich. She held it to her lips and licked the apricot jam from the edge, then nibbled for a moment before stopping.

"Some water?" I picked up the glass Mr. Steinberg had given her.

"No, no," she muttered. Aunt Sally stood, went into the bedroom, shut the door, and turned the latch. My basket, with the last of Grandma's treats, was locked in that room too.

Alone, I looked through the parlor's lace curtain. The warm glow of lamplight shone from apartment windows across the street where families sat at their supper tables. My tummy ached. I imagined a mother ladling up bowls of steamy soup. A plate filled with slices of freshly baked bread being passed around. I could almost smell the food and hear the grown-ups laughing at the shenanigans of their children, cautioning them not to talk with their mouths full. Lost a few tears, but quickly wiped them with my fingers, determined not to weep like Aunt Sally.

Chapter 7

Mama hadn't taught me to cook yet, because she wouldn't let me near the stove. Wondered if Grandma had trained her Sally to bake. I went into the kitchen hoping to find a pie or cake or plate of cookies waiting to welcome me. Saw nothing but a bowl of pears. I opened the larder, hoping to find something for a meal, and was disappointed again—only an onion, a sack of beans, and a few raw potatoes. On the shelf were tins of sardines and a box of crackers. Didn't bother looking for a tin opener.

Instead, I searched for the apartment key. Found it on the table next to the settee. I picked up Mama's gloves, jingled the coins, then walked out to the landing. My spirits lifted. In two shakes I locked the door, pulled on the gloves, and skedaddled downstairs to look for Frank's Freshest Fish.

There weren't as many people on the street as when I first stepped into the city. That seemed forever ago. It had only been a few hours. My stomach growled. It also churned a little. The emptiness I recognized, but the other thing was different. A topsy-turvy, unsettled feeling. Not quite sick, but very unpleasant.

If I could find Frank's and buy two fresh fish, then fry them up the way Mama had done with Papa's catch on our camping trip, maybe Aunt Sally would feel better. And showing her how helpful I could be might make her less nervous. Possibly, we'd find something to like about each other. At least we could eat together.

"Young lady? Please, wait." The man's voice sounded familiar.

I looked back to see Mr. Steinberg. His long legs and quick strides had him next to me in no time.

"Sorry, I don't know your name. We weren't properly introduced," he said.

Papa says he takes the measure of a man by the grip of his handshake. So I thrust my hand out and said, "I'm Littlebeth Morgan."

Mr. Steinberg shook firmly and smiled in the friend-liest way. "Littlebeth? Appears to me you're on the verge of outgrowing that name."

"I know. Grandma called me that when I was born, and it stuck. But Aunt Sally uses my given name, Elizabeth." I scrunched up my face at the refined sound of it then went on. "It's how she would have introduced me if she'd used her manners. I suppose having the re-sponsibility of a *country girl* like me and falling on her fanny the way she did—which, Mr. Steinberg, I had nothing to do with—have been too much for her."

"Nice to meet you," he said and shook my hand again. This time he held it between both of his. The extra warmth of his touch came through Mama's gloves. First time I'd felt welcomed to San Francisco.

When he let go, I trembled.

"Goodness, you're not used to our night air." He removed his jacket and draped it over my shoulders. "Where are you going?"

When I told him, he frowned. "The wharf's quite a distance. Did Miss Morgan send you on this errand?"

"No, sir. She's disposed."

"Disposed?"

"Not herself. Not too well."

"Ah, you mean *indisposed*?"

"That's the word. The polite way of saying she cried herself into a state and put herself to bed without fixing supper."

"Oh dear, I never meant to cause her distress." He looked at the sidewalk then back at me.

We stood near a three-globe streetlight. Its beautiful scrolled black column reminded me I was in a city. We had nothing like this back home. Mr. Steinberg stared at me without speaking. I noticed his brown eyes glistening the way eyes do when they are moist. Only twice have I seen Papa's eyes shine like they might spill over—when Mama gave birth to Joey and when he hit his thumb with the hammer while repairing the chicken coop.

There it was again, that strange churning in my stomach.

"It's not your fault," I said. "My family put me, *their* burden, onto Aunt Sally. She's never had to take care of a child before, even though she hasn't really tried yet. I think it makes her nervous and"—I searched for the right word, then chose the knitter's—"scared. Some people say I scare grown-ups."

My stomach rumbled so loudly that Mr. Steinberg heard.

"You must be starving!" He took my arm and walked me around the corner to what he called his favorite neighborhood restaurant. On the way, he told me he'd be happy to help me find Frank's Freshest Fish tomorrow.

Wasn't sure I'd like a restaurant. I'd never eaten food made by anyone other than Mama or Grandma or the ladies from our church. Yet, the smell of vittles cooking set my mouth watering when we reached Maria's Cantina. A chalkboard by the front door listed:

Homemade Chicken Enchiladas and Rice—20 cents
Chili and Cornbread—10 cents
Scrambled Eggs and Bacon with Coffee—10 cents

"Señora Sanchez!" Mr. Steinberg greeted the plump woman with a hug and kissed her cheek.

She tucked a loose strand of gray hair behind an ear and wiped her hands on a grease-stained apron. "We miss you!" she said. "Long time since I feed you."

"Too long."

"And who is this?" She looked at me.

"My neighbor's niece, Elizabeth."

I shook the señora's hand.

"Maria, I'd like your best table, please, and two large plates of your chicken enchiladas," Mr. Steinberg said.

Señora Sanchez showed us to a little wooden table near the front.

"And what will you have?" Mr. Steinberg asked me.

They chuckled at his joke.

"Actually," I said, settling into the chair and carefully removing my gloves, "I'll have two large plates too."

The señora let out a hoot and walked away. People around us chattered, clinked forks and knifes, scooted chairs. A restaurant was a noisy place.

Knowing I'd soon be eating a hot meal calmed my tummy, even though I'd never tasted an enchilada before.

"Are you going to go to school tomorrow?"

His question startled me. I'd forgotten about the Presbyterian Academy for Girls.

"No, sir. It's Easter vacation. Next week I'm supposed to start a new school here, which I think is silly, because it's so close to the end of the term, and I'm way ahead in every subject back home."

"Easter, yes, I'd forgotten."

"Forgot the Resurrection of our Savior?"

"I'm not Christian. My people, the Hebrews, celebrate Passover, not Easter."

I was starting to ask him about that when Señora

Sanchez brought out supper and set our plates in front of us. Fat enchiladas covered in melted cheese filled my eyes and had my appetite raring to go. I dug in fast.

"You're right about your aunt," he said, picking up his fork and pointing it at me. "Your Aunt Sally is afraid...but not about taking care of you. She's afraid of herself."

Couldn't respond with my mouth full, but that was the most perplexing thing I'd ever heard. How could a person be afraid of herself? When it comes right down to it, you are all you truly have to depend on in this world. I knew that for certain after this week.

Mr. Steinberg and I finished our meals at the same time. Eating fast wasn't ladylike. Tried to make up for that by carefully cleaning my face with the napkin and folding it neatly on the table.

"Superb," I said. Knew from Mama's magazines that hoity-toities used that word for things they considered first-rate. Wanted to show him I wasn't a country hick, that I could be as proper as any city lady.

He looked surprised and smiled. "I think it's time we get you back."

We waved good-bye to Señora Sanchez. Before we'd walked half a block, I burped—a loud one.

"Did you know," Mr. Steinberg said quickly, "in the Eskimo culture that's considered a compliment to your host? A sign you enjoyed the meal."

Waited for him to say, "But you're no Eskimo, and girls in California don't belch." But he simply grinned at me.

"Golly, that's my kind of culture!" I said.

We laughed as we turned the corner and headed up the street toward his shop. "Thank you, Mr. Steinberg. I did enjoy the meal."

After a few steps, I asked him about Passover.

"It's the celebration of God freeing my people from slavery in Egypt. Do you know the story of Moses leading the Israelites out of Pharaoh's land?"

"Sure," I said, "it's in the Bible." I remembered Reverend Douglas preaching from Exodus. "I liked the part about the Lord telling Moses to lift his staff over the water and how the sea parted so the people could get away from Pharaoh's soldiers."

Mr. Steinberg nodded. "Your Easter and our Passover both happen in the spring, but our holiday is much older than yours."

He walked faster. I practically had to run to keep up.

Ahead of us, a woman stood on the sidewalk in front

of our building's staircase. She clutched a dark shawl with a tight fist against her chest. Thick auburn waves fell over her shoulders, swirling as she turned to look one way then the other. The woman spotted us, and I realized it was Aunt Sally.

I hadn't recognized her. Freed from the bun, her hair was a spectacular sight. She didn't seem so scrawny with that full mane bouncing as she came to meet us. The determination of her stride and furrow in her brow sent Mr. Steinberg stumbling over an explanation.

He repeated *starving* three times. "The child's stomach roared. Honestly, I've never heard such a noise. Naturally, I felt I had to do something. She said you'd retired for the evening. Please, Miss Morgan, don't—"

"How could you?" Aunt Sally pulled my arm. The streetlamp caught her in a most flattering way.

I was dumbstruck. Not because she was upset—I was already used to that—but because her appearance had my eyes popping. Had to remember to blink.

Her cheeks rosy and full, her eyes a glittery sea-green, her radiant locks—how could she have been so pitiful half an hour ago and glow like this now?

"Aunt Sally, you're pretty!"

"What?" She seemed as shocked as me.

"Your niece is right, dear lady. Miss Morgan." Mr. Steinberg removed his bowler and held the brim with fidgeting hands. His mouth still open even though he'd finished speaking.

"Mama says sometimes everyone needs a good cry, but I never believed it until now, because you must have had yourself the best cry a person could possibly have!"

"How dare—"

"Please don't be angry." Mr. Steinberg gently moved me to the side. He stood toe to toe with my aunt.

I thought he might embrace her for an enchanted kiss. Perhaps he would be transformed from Mr. Steinberg, the haberdasher, into a handsome prince.

Aunt Sally slapped his face with an open hand. "You had no right to take this child!" Her mouth tightened, her cheeks hollowed, and the color faded.

She would have dragged me up the steps if I hadn't had the weight of a full enchilada and obstinacy on my side. Grandma says I'm the most obstinate girl in Paso Robles, which I suppose is another reason I was sent here. Knew stubborn could be irritating. But spiteful, well, that's next to evil in my mind. Anyone as mean as Aunt Sally had nothing to teach me.

"Let go!" I twisted, jerked free of her, and ran back to

Mr. Steinberg. "I won't stay with her."

"It's all right," he said.

"I want to go home! Take me to the train depot. Please," I cried and wrapped my arms around his waist. He tensed.

"Come now, it's late." He put his hands on my shoulders. "Everything will be fine in the morning. You'll see." His voice was soft.

I felt the chill of Aunt Sally behind me. Mr. Steinberg tried to move me away from him, but I strengthened my hold.

"She hit you. She's horrible." I yelled the word, liking how it felt as I slung it at her. "Horrible!"

"Stop," he said firmly. "You don't know what you're saying. You don't understand. Stop this now." He changed his stance, bent a little, and said in a gentler tone, "It's been a long day. Everyone's tired."

Before I knew what had happened, he lifted and carried me up the stairs.

Aunt Sally opened her apartment door. He put me on the settee.

"I'm sorry, Mr. Steinberg," Aunt Sally said, her eyes on me, not him.

"I know." He left, closing the door behind him.

My aunt knelt and put her thin hand on my knee. "We've had a bad start. Tomorrow, we'll begin anew."

"How?" I took off the gloves and set them on the side table. "You don't like me, and I don't like you." Honesty was another of my faults. I stood. Mr. Steinberg's jacket fell off my shoulders.

I'd forgotten he'd put it on me. Aunt Sally and I grabbed for it at the same time. We each tugged on the garment. I let go, knowing full well she'd lose her balance, which she did. But she didn't fall, only wavered, steadied herself, and draped the jacket over her arm. Something fell from the pocket. I snatched it off the floor—a ticket for *Carmen* at the Grand Opera House on April 17, tomorrow night.

"En-rico Ca-ruso." I sounded out the name. "Who is he?"

"Caruso is the greatest tenor in the world," Aunt Sally said, holding out her palm. "Now give me that."

"It's Mr. Steinberg's. I'm returning it to him." I ran for the door.

She got there first, put her back against it, and faced me. "We will return his belongings in the morning." A flush of color appeared on her cheeks. "He opens his establishment at the same time I open mine."

"Fine, but I'll keep this." I gripped the opera ticket, took it to the bedroom, and put it inside my basket for safekeeping.

I returned for Mama's gloves. Fished around for my aunt's apartment key. Gave it back to her without speaking. She watched me pull out the key for Papa's trunk and followed me into the bedroom. I unlocked the padlock, opened the lid, and found my best nightgown folded on top. Then I dragged the cot into the parlor, not wanting to sleep in the same room with her. She didn't seem to mind.

That churning feeling came back as I lay on the cot. In the dark, I realized what it was. Homesickness. Missed my family something awful.

Couldn't stay here. Had to go home. Hoped Mr. Steinberg would be so grateful to get his opera ticket back he'd help me by taking me to the train station tomorrow.

The fact my family didn't want me was a problem I'd have to work out. Maybe I could pretend to be refined until they got used to me again.

Wondered how Mr. Steinberg—someone so different than me, a city man I'd just met who didn't believe in Easter but sure knew how to follow the Golden Rule—could be nicer to me than my own kin. A true friend.

Fell asleep wishing Papa could meet Mr. Steinberg. Wanted him to know there was someone, a grown-up, who liked me for me.

Chapter 8

Tuesday, April 17, 1906

"Wake up. Your breakfast is on the table." Aunt Sally jiggled my shoulder. She sounded chipper. A happy new start for her.

But not for me.

That little cot had turned into a cozy cradle. Pulled the blanket over my head and tried to return to my dream of running through a barley field chasing...Who was I chasing?

"Up, now! Eat and wash," Aunt Sally said, plucking off my cover. "I open the shop in an hour." She shook and folded the blanket in quick order.

I groaned, struggled upright, and squinted at the gaslight on the wall. Not enough sun yet from the window to feel like morning. Aunt Sally's face came into focus. Her magnificent hair had been pulled back, pinned into a bun. Restrained.

Shuffling to the table, I sat where a white bowl waited for me. Porridge. Tasted like warm paste.

"Mama gives me sweet coffee with lots of cream and warm bread with strawberry jam." I tilted the spoon to let the mush return to the bowl.

"Children shouldn't drink coffee."

"When Grandma makes oatmeal, she puts in raisins, cinnamon, and honey. Didn't she teach you how to make it like that?"

"Young ladies shouldn't think so much about their stomachs. Food is for sustenance, not pleasure." She tried to smile but couldn't hold it. "Eat up." She sat beside me, took a sip from her teacup, then sighed.

"Your grandmother did attempt to train me in cookery. I had neither the inclination to learn, nor the skill to meet her standards."

Swallowing another spoonful of porridge, I tried not to gag. "You're sure right about that, Auntie!"

She handed me a glass of milk. The corners of her mouth began to curl.

"Never thought I'd miss Grandma so much," I said,

taking a swig.

We both laughed. That surprised me so much that I snorted and milk came out of my nose.

Aunt Sally patted my back. "Stop this silliness. We have a shop to open and run." She herded me to the bathroom sink. "Today, I'll let you serve as my assistant." She made it sound like a privilege.

She stood over me while I scrubbed my face. After toweling dry, I turned to her. "How did you get your shop?" I wondered, just then, how it felt to be your own boss with no one else to answer to.

"A long story for another time," she said, leading me to her bedroom.

My curiosity had stirred the minute she laughed. Now questions popped like hot corn kernels in the pan. The knitting lady on the train said it was unusual for an unmarried woman to have a business. How had my aunt done it? And why did she live and work so far from her family? Wondered if Grandma had been as hard on her as she was on me.

"No time like the present." I smiled with what I hoped was encouragement.

She began brushing my hair, yanking out tangles. "Briefly then," she said. "When Father died, Mother sold our ranch and bought the house in Paso Robles. I was twelve and John, seventeen."

I reached back to protect my scalp. "You're pulling too hard. It hurts."

"Do you want to hear this or not?"

I nodded.

"Your bedroom was actually mine years ago."

I twisted around and stared at her. Couldn't believe *our* home belonged to Grandma and that my room had been Aunt Sally's when she was a girl. Tried to picture her at my age. Impossible.

She turned me forward then separated and interlaced strands of hair into one long braid down my back. "Mother wanted her children to have opportunities. With the money from the ranch and Father's investments, she saw to our education. John went off to Santa Clara College. He fell in love with a classmate's sister— your mother. And came home with a bride before he earned his diploma then went to work at the bank.

"When I turned fifteen, Mother sent me to finishing school at the same Presbyterian Academy for Girls you'll attend on Monday. I boarded at the school. A different experience than you'll have as a day student."

"Costs more to live at the school?" I asked.

"Yes. I needed to earn spending money, so with the help of the school, I secured employment in Madam Bouchard's shop. The one below." Aunt Sally tied a red satin bow at the end of my braid.

Told her I hated bows. She lightly smacked my bottom with the back of the hairbrush.

"I may not cook well, but I do know what looks well on ladies."

"Sorry, Auntie."

"As Madam Bouchard's protégée, I mastered the fine art of providing a lady with the perfect accessories for her person and her home." She pointed to the bench in front of her dressing table. "Sit." She handed me my white stockings and garters.

"But how did it become your shop?" I pulled up the long socks.

"Madam was an older woman," she said. "A widow with no children. She depended entirely upon me. I stayed on after graduation as her assistant. Sadly the influenza took her a few years later, but she provided for me."

Aunt Sally had just said more words to me than I'd heard from her since she met me at the train station. And I was starting to get interested in her.

"She gave you her shop?" I walked over to the wardrobe where she held out my outfit on a hanger.

"Bequeathed it to me, as she would have to her kin, if she'd had any. I've built up the clientele, established a good reputation. Last year, I changed the name of the shop to my own." Heard the pride in her voice and grinned at her. Had a hundred more questions.

"No more talk," she said.

Aunt Sally had chosen my navy skirt and white blouse with the wide sailor collar for me to wear. In that getup, I looked like little Buster Brown. Found myself doubting her fashion skills.

Papa loved Buster in the newspaper's Sunday funnies. Always read that one to us first after church. He made his voice gruff to exaggerate the errors of Buster's mischief and finished with a chuckle, saying, "Thank goodness that boy has Tige to watch over him."

I had a different opinion. I thought a *good* dog would run and fetch and follow Buster Brown on adventures, not fold his paws like arms, turn up his snout, then preach a short sermon about doing right to be right. What kid would want a dog like Tige? Reckoned Papa wanted a mutt like that trailing after me.

Aunt Sally put on her hat and coat, even though we

only had to go down the stairs, turn right, and walk four paces to her shop. She had her purse on her arm. "Come, Elizabeth. Chatting has made us late."

"You've forgotten Mr. Steinberg's jacket," I said, remembering my plan to have my new friend help me.

I went back into the bedroom before she could protest. His jacket hung in the wardrobe. Grabbed it and my basket with the opera ticket inside. Noticed there was one biscuit left. I ate it in three quick bites. Not as soft as yesterday, but it still tasted like home. Thought about how I'd ask Mr. Steinberg for a favor once I returned his ticket.

"Let's not dawdle," I said, racing to the front door with the jacket over my arm and the basket in hand. If Mr. Steinberg put me on the southbound train today, I'd have about seven hours to figure out how to convince my family to let me live with them again.

Passed my aunt on the stairs, and hurried to Mr. Steinberg's shop. I saw him through the window. He was standing behind the counter showing a pair of white gloves to a gentleman. I opened the door and strode past displays of bowlers, fedoras, boaters, and Panama hats. Went by shelves of stiff white collars, bow ties, and suspenders.

"You forgot your jacket and your ticket to *Carmen*, but I have them for you," I said to Mr. Steinberg.

"One moment, please." He gave me the look I've seen on every grown-up's face I know. The wait-your-turn, wait-until-I-have-time, wait-wait-wait look. No matter how important what you have to say is, grown-ups don't want to hear it until they are good and ready.

If only that worked for children, we'd never have to hear things like: Do your sums. Do your chores. Wash behind your ears. Go to bed.

That would be a dandy how-do-you-do.

"Going to *Carmen* is the reason I need these fancy things. My wife insists." The man pulled off the glove he'd tried on.

"May I wrap these, sir?" Mr. Steinberg made neat corners on the brown paper, then tied the small package with string.

"Quite the night for our fair city, eh, little girl?" The gentleman smiled at me. "The great Caruso serenades the Barbary bandits!"

"That will be two dollars," said Mr. Steinberg.

The man lost his smile, paid, and bumped into me on his way out the door.

Aunt Sally was rooted near the entrance, not venturing

a foot forward. I'd hoped she would go directly to her shop so I could be alone with Mr. Steinberg.

"Good morning, Miss Morgan." He came around his counter.

She nodded in his direction, but her eyes were fastened on me. "Elizabeth, come. I must open for my customers."

"Go ahead. Just be a minute," I said, clutching my basket and Mr. Steinberg's jacket.

"That fellow was waiting at the door for me," he said to Aunt Sally. "But there's no one about now." He held his hand out, beckoning her to come in. "You know what a historic event Caruso's performance will be. I beg you to reconsider. Sharing an evening of opera isn't—"

"It's not possible." Aunt Sally shook her head.

I watched them, tried to figure out what was going on.

"I have an alternative suggestion." Mr. Steinberg took a step toward her.

"This is neither the place nor time." She held her ground.

"My friend in the orchestra tells me people are clamoring for tickets," he said, "but none are to be had. He says if I turn mine into the theater by noon, we'll be allowed into the gallery for the last rehearsal. And we can take your niece. Think of it—Enrico Caruso for lunch! There would be no impropriety."

Mr. Steinberg took the jacket from my arm, rummaged through the pockets and retrieved a single ticket. He looked concerned.

That puzzled me until I realized he expected to find two tickets. Then I understood. He was sweet on my aunt and had bought them each a ticket, but she clearly didn't want to step out with him.

I took the extra ticket from my basket and handed it to him. It had lost its power. If we spent the afternoon listening to Caruso practice his opera, I couldn't ask Mr. Steinberg to take me to the train depot. He might not have done it anyway. He was a grown-up after all. Maybe he only liked me so he could get close to my aunt.

"I don't know," she said. "Yesterday I had to close the shop early to meet Elizabeth."

Mr. Steinberg crossed the distance to her and said, "We could close our shops for a two-hour lunch, then stay open an hour later tonight. And take no lunch break tomorrow."

His brown eyes looked so gosh-darn hopeful that I felt sorry for him. Couldn't stop myself. I tried to rescue the poor fella.

"Auntie," I said, "You know I'd never see someone as famous as Mr. Caruso at home. The last entertainment we had was the volunteer firemen's rope-pulling contest in the park with the high school band playing John Philip Sousa marches. The Ladies' Auxiliary sold slices of peach pie and passed out temperance leaflets, which was a waste of time because all the firemen drank buckets of beer after their contest and used the leaflets to wipe their mouths after eating the pie. Did you know Papa's team won? And Mama didn't speak to him at supper because his team celebrated too much, and she's the treasurer of the Ladies' Auxiliary."

Now I had their attention. And it looked like I'd almost convinced Aunt Sally. Saving other people never did me any good. If she agreed to go, I'd have to come up with a brand-new plan to get home.

She took a moment to consider, while Mr. Steinberg practically held his breath waiting for a yes. My brain whirred.

The sooner Aunt Sally gave me some big-city culture, the better for both of us. Figured opera counted for a heaping mound of ladylike refinement. She might even ship me home early. If that didn't work, at least Mr. Steinberg could see I'd helped him out. I hoped he'd be honor bound to return the favor when I needed it.

Besides, now Mr. Caruso had my curiosity. I wanted to hear what greatness sounded like.

Chapter 9

The Grand Opera House fit its name. It occupied an entire block on Mission Street. Sets of arched doors marked the entrance—tall enough for a man with a dozen top hats stacked on his head to walk through with room to spare. Looked like a home for giants.

Mr. Steinberg led us toward two open ticket windows near those fancy doors. Lines formed at each one. We stood at the end of the shortest line. Nine people were ahead of us. The other line was five times as long and went back to the curb then wound down the block. A woman walked away from our window after returning two *Carmen* tickets for a refund. She dabbed her eyes with a hankie.

Was going to tell Aunt Sally the handkerchiefs she sold in her shop were nicer than that woman's, when the first man in the long line shouted, "I'll take her tickets!"

Mumbling spread from the people behind him, all the way back to where the line curved along the sidewalk. It was plain to see most of those folks weren't going to get tickets for tonight's performance, with so few people in our line.

Sold Out signs were pasted over Mr. Caruso's profile on all the *Carmen* posters around the opera house. Two police officers stood off to the side, keeping an eye on things. I asked why, and Mr. Steinberg told me they had to make sure people in our line didn't try to profit by selling their tickets directly to the eager folks in the other line for more than the theater would charge, which I figured was plenty.

Wondered how much Mr. Steinberg had paid to spend an evening with my aunt. Now he had to settle for a lunchtime outing with me tagging along. He looked happy enough though. Even Aunt Sally had an air of anticipation about her as we made our way up to the window. Finally Mr. Steinberg traded in his tickets so we could see the rehearsal.

Instead of money, the cashier gave us each a piece

of paper he'd stamped with an official-looking seal and told us to join a small group gathered by the big doors. A man in wire-rimmed spectacles poked his head out from behind the middle door. He gestured for us to come inside. We gathered around him in the lobby.

He adjusted the sleeve of his gray suit. "You are the fortunate few," he said.

Aunt Sally whispered to Mr. Steinberg, "I'm surprised more people didn't choose this option."

A woman wearing a blue felt hat with a green feather sticking up on the side looked over and said, "Tonight's tickets are so precious only fools or invalids would give them up."

"Which are you?" I asked.

Aunt Sally and Mr. Steinberg exhaled my name at the same time.

The woman laughed. "Asked for that, I suppose, but not your place to point it out, dearie." She poked my shoulder twice with her finger, knocking me back a step and putting me in my place, and went on. "My husband, the old fool, broke his leg falling off a ladder yesterday. So you could say he's in both categories." She smiled at me. "My sister is the seamstress here and told me about the rehearsal, or I'd have lost my chance to hear the wonderful Caruso altogether."

A fellow behind us volunteered that his wife's mother had had a stroke last night but was too mean to die. A few ladies snapped their tongues at him. Having been in the same position seconds before, I felt sorry for him. He said his son was a stagehand.

The man in the gray suit walked to the foot of the widest, fanciest staircase in creation. Polished wood and gold-trimmed molding framed everything around us. He went up the first step, turned, and waved for us to follow. Looking at me, the man said, "Children are not normally allowed."

Mr. Steinberg assured him I had permission to be there, mentioning his musician friend's name. "First chair oboe," he added.

The guide lowered his chin and gave me the grown-up look. "No giggling. No talking."

"Yes, sir. I mean, no, sir." I tried to curtsy but wavered when I dipped. Aunt Sally put her arm through mine to steady me.

As we climbed the magenta-carpeted stairs, Mr. Steinberg leaned near to say, "This is one of the largest, best-appointed opera houses in the entire United States."

I rubbed the shiny banister. What a fun ride this

would be. Mr. Steinberg must have guessed my thought because he winked at me.

Aunt Sally squeezed close. For an instant I wondered if she too shared the idea of sliding down full-speed.

"Think of all the elegantly dressed ladies and gentlemen who have stood on these very steps over the years," she said.

Her imaginings were different from mine. A hint of girlishness flickered across her face. I reckoned she pictured herself wearing a fine evening gown with strings of pearls around her neck and carrying a small fan in her gloved hand. A dashing escort on her arm. A dream she could have lived if she'd only agreed to see the opera tonight with Mr. Steinberg.

Even if he was in a tuxedo, I doubted my aunt would consider him dashing. He was what Mama called pleasantly homely—a person you wouldn't look at twice if he were a stranger, but if you knew and admired him, you were always pleased to see his face.

"This evening," the guide said, "our audience, including the city's elite, will be elbow to elbow for Signore Caruso's performance as Don Jose, and, of course, Madam Olive Fremstad as Carmen." He spread his hands wide in front of his chest, continuing, "Every one of the 2,400 seats in the house will be filled."

"Golly, that's more folks than we have in my town!" The words flew from my mouth.

I stiffened, expecting Aunt Sally to shush or scold me. But the gilded mirror on the wall reflected her turning this way and that, taking in the full splendor of the place. She hadn't heard me, didn't even notice people twittering. Her attention rested on the crystal chandelier overhead. Daylight caught its long prisms to cast off colorful patterns against the brocade wallpaper. I realized she was as awed by all this as I'd been when I first experienced the hubbub of the city.

Maybe we had more in common than Grandma and Papa and the same bedroom.

"Young lady, over four hundred thousand people live in San Francisco," the guide said. He opened a door and directed us to the balcony, saying, "Our culture rivals the great cities back east."

Mr. Steinberg carefully led the way down steep steps to the front chairs. He and Aunt Sally took a seat on either side of me. I remained on my feet, putting my hands on the railing and leaning over for a bird's-eye view. The rows below us were covered in drop cloths.

"Did they paint the ceiling?" I asked Mr. Steinberg.

"That's to protect the upholstered chairs from dust," he said. "When people arrive tonight in all their finery, they'll place their rumps on clean cushions."

I giggled, caught myself, and looked for the guide. Aunt Sally frowned. Luckily the man had gone.

Members of the orchestra began taking their places in the pit below the stage. When he saw his pal, Mr. Steinberg nudged me.

Wanted to wave at the man but decided I'd better not. That might get my friend or his or me into trouble.

"Will we be able to hear Mr. Caruso over the sound of all those fiddles and horns, drums and cymbals?" I asked, still looking over the railing.

"Of course," a woman said behind me.

Aunt Sally tugged my skirt until I dropped into the wooden seat. No drop cloths up here.

Purple velvet curtains were drawn across the stage. "Extravagant, aren't they?" Aunt Sally said.

Wondered if the famous tenor would stand in front of them to compete with the musicians. Reckoned Mr. Caruso must be a huge man to need such a big house to sing in.

"Ladies and gentlemen." The man in the gray suit now stood on the main floor in front of the orchestra.

He cupped his hands around his mouth to project his voice up to us. "Because the demand to see Signore Caruso is overwhelming," he said, "the maestro has graciously opened this rehearsal to you. A rare opportunity. Absolute silence is required. No talking or applause. Think of yourselves as flies on the wall, observing, careful not to draw attention, lest you be promptly dispatched."

Aunt Sally pinched my arm. "Not one word!"

I raised my eyebrows at her—she'd just said three!

Mr. Steinberg also ignored the no-talking rule by whispering to me, "This is Georges Bizet's masterpiece. It's set in Seville, Spain."

His *s*'s tickled my ear. I struggled not to laugh.

The guide went on. "You won't see the entire opera, but you will hear portions of the arias. A final note: Signore Caruso is courageously entertaining us despite the recent eruption of Mount Vesuvius near his hometown of Naples, Italy, and the terrible news that the volcano has claimed hundreds of lives. While his heart is with his countrymen, he honors his commitments. We are grateful to him. Our prayers are with the victims."

Caterwauling screeches of strings and horns being tuned echoed through the theater. I wanted to hear more about that deadly volcano, but the guide retreated.

Mr. Steinberg again whispered in my ear. "Caruso plays a soldier named Don Jose, who sees the gypsy Carmen on her lunch break from the cigarette factory. Her beauty steals his heart. He deserts his post to be with her, but she loses interest and pledges her love to another. When she's confronted by the rejected Don Jose, she's defiant, and their fates are sealed."

Started to whisper back, but he held a finger to his lips and shook his head. I'd have to ask later about *sealed fates*.

Behind the curtain, a woman squealed then yelled. Aunt Sally looked from me to Mr. Steinberg. He raised his eyebrows. Don't think any of us expected opera to be such a painful noise.

Men in overalls pulled back the curtain. Onstage, wooden panels were cut and painted to look like buildings around a Spanish square. A hefty woman with a voice to match shook her fist at a man holding a hammer.

"Idiot!" she hollered. The poor fellow hung his shoulders and backed away. She used words I didn't know. Curse words, I figured, from all the slouching and squirming in the seats around me.

Sounds from the orchestra dwindled as her rage

grew. A man behind us said, "She's carrying on like a stuck pig."

"That's Carmen," a woman whispered.

"But she's not beautiful," I said aloud, earning a smack on my thigh from Aunt Sally.

"Sure wouldn't tempt me, little miss," said the man behind us. He patted the top of my head.

Aunt Sally gave us both stern glares.

We all inhaled at the same time when Mr. Caruso appeared. He looked just like his picture—a bushy shock of dark hair and portly. But I was shocked to see how short he was. Not nearly as tall as Mr. Steinberg.

His hands moved as he spoke to the woman, too softly for us to hear. He seemed to calm her. "Okay," he boomed. "All is okay!" He nodded at the crew on the far end of the stage then turned to the conductor and motioned to begin.

The famous Caruso strode to center stage then let out the fullest, most peculiar, yet perfect sound I'd ever heard. Music from the pit filtered in beneath his tones.

Mr. Steinberg barely whispered, "'The Flower Song.'" His face beamed.

For a moment, I stared at Mr. Steinberg, enjoying his pleasure at hearing Caruso while near Aunt Sally. Made me happy that I'd helped him. Thought there must be something nice about my aunt to make a man like him want to spend time with her.

Then the tenor's voice captured me. It unfurled like a bolt of rich silk floating over the stage—higher and higher it went, until it dipped thrillingly low, then rose again. It filled all the space inside this grand theater. His voice *was* gigantic, even if he was not.

Hairs on my neck and arms tingled and stood straight up. My heart raced to hold the notes, to ride the current of the melody. Closed my eyes, stretched my ears wide, and listened with my whole body. When he finished, I had to suck air into my lungs. Nothing had ever taken my breath away like the magical sound of Mr. Caruso's voice.

Chapter 10

On our way home, Mr. Steinberg insisted on taking us to a fancy ice cream and soda parlor for a treat. There were dozens of small, round, marble-topped tables surrounded by dainty, white wrought-iron chairs with smiling people in them, sitting close, heads bowed over their desserts. Behind a long counter, shelves full of sparkling glassware in different sizes and shapes sat ready for sodas, malts, egg creams, ice cream, or sundaes.

Oh, I wanted one of everything. My excitement grew as a man with a handlebar mustache and a long, white apron tied around his waist showed us to an empty table. I was about to ask how many scoops of chocolate and vanilla ice cream I could have when Mr. Steinberg told the man we'd have three root beers, and that would be all.

I moaned, but nobody noticed. Aunt Sally couldn't stop talking about the opulence of the opera house. Mr. Steinberg nodded and grinned. She took a sip of her drink, which gave me a chance to ask him about Don Jose and Carmen's fate being sealed.

"Don Jose kills Carmen because he can't have her, and he pays the price for his crime," he said. "Do you remember 'The Flower Song'?"

"Of course," I said, feeling goose bumps all over again.

"The opera is in French so I know you didn't understand the words, but I could recite the gist of the song in English if you like."

"Yes," Aunt Sally said before I could.

Mr. Steinberg cleared his throat and began:

In prison I kept lovingly
The flower you had thrown at me.
Though it had faded and turned dry,
It still smelled sweet as time went by;
...I only felt but one desire,
But one desire, one hope, one yen,
To see you, Carmen, yes, see you again!

Mr. Steinberg noticed people at other tables watching

him. "I'm sorry," he said to my aunt. "The passion of the piece—my voice carries."

Aunt Sally sputtered into her straw, coughed, and tried to catch her breath. I slapped her on the back.

"Must have gone down wrong," I said.

She blotted her mouth with the napkin, gave me a withering look, then said, "This has been an exceptional diversion. Thank you, Mr. Steinberg. However, we need to get back to our shops."

We didn't talk on the trolley ride home. But I caught Mr. Steinberg looking at my aunt when she wasn't stealing glimpses of him. Held on to my bonnet as we rounded a corner and thought how Aunt Sally seemed kinder today. Had her heart softened? Mr. Caruso's fine singing and Mr. Steinberg's understanding of the opera story had surely made as favorable an impression on her as they had on me. Maybe she'd appreciate the hat-seller's refined taste in music enough to let him woo her. The notion of their romance set me calculating.

Even though Mr. Steinberg owed me a favor, I wasn't as anxious as I'd been last night to ask him to take me to the train depot. And watching him admire my aunt, I realized he wouldn't put me on a train without talking to her first. That would be the end of that.

Unless I used trickery. A small fib in the good cause of a child trying to return home. Yet, even a small lie could be considered a sin. Might not count, though, if Mr. Steinberg's people didn't believe in sin. Before I got comfortable with that, another thought came. The fib wouldn't be for a good cause. My family didn't want me back. At least, not until I'd been changed into a proper young lady.

Closed my eyes, felt the rush of air wash over me as we moved along. Heard Papa's voice in my head. "Right is right and wrong is wrong, no matter what church or political party you do or don't belong to." He said that every time he read something that offended him in the newspaper. Pursed my lips to stop the quiver that happened every time I thought of Papa. But his words rang true.

Lying to Mr. Steinberg could never be right. He'd just taken me to the most beautiful place I'd ever seen. Nothing back home compared to the Grand Opera House. And truly, Mr. Caruso had the greatest voice I'd ever heard.

Why did I even want to go back to a family that sent me away? To show them they were wrong—make them sorry—but I was the sorry one, aching for home, for them.

Aunt Sally didn't seem so bad today, and maybe we could get along. And San Francisco, with its wonders to explore, might be the perfect place for me after all. My aunt believed it was the right place for her. I opened my eyes to the golden city and took a deep breath of the possibilities it held.

Best of all, if Mr. Steinberg won Aunt Sally's affections, she'd spend more time with him and have less interest in refining me.

When we left the trolley, I had an idea. "Auntie," I said, "after work, can we go to Frank's Freshest Fish?"

She looked at me as if I'd asked the strangest thing.

"We could make fish stew for dinner and invite Mr. Steinberg over to thank him for today." I was tickled with myself for thinking up such a good plan.

She gave me a quick shake of her head. Mr. Steinberg kept his eyes forward and acted like he hadn't heard me.

Then I remembered my aunt couldn't cook. She was probably embarrassed about that.

As we walked downhill toward our building, I had another idea. Putting myself between Aunt Sally and Mr. Steinberg, I pushed my foot forward on the sidewalk so that the smooth sole of my shoe slid like a skate on ice. I grabbed their hands for balance. "These hills aren't safe with slippery shoes. Be careful, Auntie."

Dropping their hands, I shifted to the outside of Mr. Steinberg, and said to him, "You should probably take her arm."

"You're the one who needs to watch her step, Elizabeth," Aunt Sally said in a tone that might have been joking or could have been scolding.

Mr. Steinberg laughed and, being a gentleman, took my aunt's arm.

She immediately removed her arm from his. My stomach lurched a little, because clearly Mr. Steinberg wore his heart on his sleeve, and she'd just brushed it off.

"Thank you for taking us to the opera rehearsal, Mr. Steinberg." I talked fast, tried to cushion his feelings. "I think you are about the nicest man I've ever met, and if I were a lady your age, I'd want you to be my beau."

His cheeks blushed so red, it hurt me to see. "Good day," he said, tipping his hat. Then he hurried to unlock his shop door.

"Elizabeth." It sounded like a hiss.

I planted my feet. Braced myself for Aunt Sally's sharp tongue to cut into me.

"You have embarrassed Mr. Steinberg and me." The sad, quiet way she spoke startled me.

"What do you mean?"

My aunt unlocked her shop and flipped the sign in the window to Open. She ignored my question but took my bonnet and put it behind the sales counter with her hat, coat, and purse. "Just straighten the tablecloths," she said, "and shake out the lace doilies then stack them again."

Couldn't understand her. This morning she'd laughed and talked to me. And I knew she'd enjoyed the opera house, but now she was back to being mean. Never wanted to be that kind of refined lady. Too confusing.

A woman came in, browsed through the lace collars, and chatted with my aunt about the good weather. I fidgeted. The woman tried on four fancy yokes. The choice between narrow or wide, scalloped or V-shaped, seem to weigh on her like a monumental decision.

Aunt Sally recommended one the lady hadn't tried on yet. She draped it under the woman's neck, then held up the mirror. "This suits your face better."

When the customer made her purchase and left, I blurted out, "Mr. Steinberg loves you. Why can't you at least be kind to him?"

Aunt Sally sighed and looked at me a few seconds before speaking. "He has tested the limits of our cordiality." She picked up a feather duster and walked to the center display table. Swishing the duster over the wooden top, she said, "Today you encouraged him to pursue something neither of us...that he cannot..."

She put a finger under her nose, sniffed as if holding in a sneeze, and turned away. With a teary catch in her throat, she said, "It's hard for me too."

"Auntie, do you like him?"

"It's impossible," she said. "He's Jewish. There can be no courting, no marriage."

"That's silly. Mama's a Methodist, and Papa's a Presbyterian. Didn't stop them from getting married."

"Differences between Protestants are not the same as completely different religions."

"I don't understand."

"Which is why you must stay out of it!" Her voice rose and she shook the duster at me. Sighing, she came closer. "I'm sorry," she said. "It's complicated. People of different faiths, who don't believe the same things, don't—"

"He told me Hebrews don't celebrate Easter. But I could teach him how, if that would help," I said.

"No, it wouldn't. His faith says Jesus is not the Messiah, not the Son of God. How could we be together? Have children? Where would they worship?

Society wouldn't accept us." She blew her nose on one of her fine hankies. "We will never speak of this again."

* * *

After a supper of sardines on crackers and pear slices for dessert, Aunt Sally took to her bed. I lay on my cot in the parlor, thinking how unfair love could be. How miserable it made people. Like Don Jose and Carmen, Mr. Steinberg and Aunt Sally. Even my own family didn't love me enough to keep me at home.

Chapter 11

Wednesday, April 18, 1906

I was in the same barley field I'd dreamed of the night before. Tender shafts brushed against my bare legs as I ran. But my feet caught more air than ground—they flapped uselessly. I pushed deeper into the dream, determined to gain purchase, to catch the shadow ahead of me. It looked like a boy. The boy from the train?

Became aware of being shaken. Didn't want Aunt Sally waking me before I caught up and found out if it was him. That boy. Tom. Sank my feet into the earth.

Somewhere below, a giant's ferocious growl rose as he clawed his way up, up through the dirt and rolled his huge body across the barley, crushing the grain. He stood, shook himself off. His gyrations sent me hurtling to the parlor floor. Smacked my head. Dazed, I wondered if I'd jumped off the cot to escape the nightmare.

Before I could cipher it out, I found myself bouncing and banging across the parlor floor alongside figurines, candlesticks, and chairs. Glass crashed and shattered. Plaster cracked. Pieces of the ceiling fell. I covered my head.

Roaring jolts shook the walls, making them move in and out like a heaving chest. Floorboards rocked so violently I couldn't get off my hands and knees. Through the grinding and rattling, I heard a scream.

"Aunt Sally!"

I crawled toward her bedroom, hesitating with each buck of the floor. Doorjambs twisted and snapped. Cupboard doors opened, and dishes flew out. Sounded like a train crashing through the building. Tucked myself into a kneeling position, arms over my head, and prayed for the mayhem to stop. When I looked up, the bedroom door, ripped from its top hinge, hung crookedly. Through the open space, dust swirled.

"Aunt Sally!"

No answer. Another shuddering jolt sent me sliding into the chest of drawers—thrown facedown across the bedroom threshold. Held on to it for an anchor in the roiling torrent. Took a few shaky breaths before I peered over the bureau. Nothing was where it belonged. I blinked away dust clouds to see better.

Half the room had vanished. The princess bed was gone. The outside wall not there at all. Felt like I was inside an eerie dollhouse facing a dark, broken world.

"Auntie! Answer me."

She wasn't there. Everything inside me tightened. Had to get out before the rest of the building crumbled, before I disappeared like poor Aunt Sally.

I scooted back into the parlor, realized the shaking had slowed. That instant, the frenzy began anew. The clatter grew louder, faster until the jolting rattled me so hard I feared I'd lose teeth.

The floor shifted and rolled me into the settee. I used its armrest to pull myself upright. First time on my feet since I'd been thrown from the cot. Standing steady, I didn't trust that the movement had stopped. Waited, listened. Silence.

The front door, knocker side up, was lying flat on the parlor rug like it had been kicked in. Plaster dust hurt my eyes. I rubbed them and squinted. Looked down at a shard of blue glass, suspended in the thick air. Blinked, looked again. The glass had pierced the top of my bare foot and stuck straight up. Red droplets formed at its base, dripping down my skin in thin, wiggly lines.

I squatted and pulled the piece out, dabbed the blood with the bottom of my nightgown. Felt no pain. Staring at it, I recognized it was from the vase that held the daffodils. Looked for the flowers, but only saw shattered, sharp things strewn about—waiting to cut me. Made my way to the overturned cot, found one shoe. Spotted the other under the dining table.

Saw something yellow, but the haze blurred my vision. Shoved my feet into the shoes. Had to get out.

Crossing over the front door, I stumbled on loose bricks and shreds of wall plaster scattered around the landing. The section connecting Aunt Sally's and Mr. Steinberg's apartments looked like it had been squeezed together, then pulled apart.

Mr. Steinberg! Had he met the same fate as Aunt Sally? Shouted his name. Peered through the blur of crushed bricks and mortar. His front door, torn from its hinges, laid sideways, letting me see into his parlor. Parts of the ceiling, bricks, and strips of wood formed a pile inside.

Yelled for him again.

"I'm trapped!" His voice sounded hoarse and frightened.

"I hear you but can't see you," I called.

He didn't answer. The silence scared me more than the thunderous quaking. Had trouble catching my breath. When I inhaled, I tasted lime and sand.

Easing a foot forward, I looked up to open sky. Below me were pieces of the roof. Chunks of our building had tumbled over the edge of the landing. Between our apartments, where the staircase should have been, was an open gap, too wide to jump.

"There's a hole between us," I shouted. "The stairs and part of the landing are gone."

Waited, then tried again. "Mr. Steinberg?"

There'd only been one scream from Aunt Sally before half her bedroom ripped away. Imagined her, in that pretty bed, falling to the ground. Closed my eyes tight and opened them again, hoping the world would be normal. Didn't work. I saw an arm sticking out of the rubble pile in Mr. Steinberg's parlor.

My knees buckled.

"Here," he called. "I'm here!" His hand lifted and moved in a pitiful wave.

"Hold on," I said, breathing fast. "I'll find a way to you."

I went back through our apartment to what was left of the bedroom. Thought the shared wall between Aunt

Sally's and his place might have shaken enough to split it open so I could get through to him.

I climbed over the bureau. Saw a heap of wreckage where the dressing table should have been. Wondered if my aunt could have been thrown from her bed like I'd been from the cot, if she could be trapped under the rubble like Mr. Steinberg.

This time I screamed, "Aunt Sally!"

No response. No limbs sticking out. Made myself look at the side wall. Couldn't find any fractures to push my way through. Couldn't get to Mr. Steinberg from here.

Thought of the man at the opera house who said Mr. Caruso's hometown in Italy had been devastated by a volcano. Maybe that catastrophe had traveled across the ocean to hit us. Maybe we were the last ones to face the end.

The end. It seized my heart. The end of everything?

"Mama!" I cried. My insides shook like the apartment had moments ago. "Papa!"

Pictured our house in Paso Robles collapsing on top of my family. Joey's little arm sticking out of the debris. My chest hurt like I was the one trapped under the weight of beams and bricks. Couldn't breathe, couldn't move. "Mama!" I cried again, knowing she wasn't there.

"Hey! Up there—little girl!"

Braced myself against the wall dividing the apartments, sidled over to within a few feet of the end of the jagged floor, and looked down. On the street, a man stared up. His trouser suspenders covered bare shoulders. He called to me again. I managed to nod at him but couldn't speak.

"Stay where you are!" He said then ran off.

My eyes watered. I tried to breathe in and out, slowly. Put my mouth next to the wall and shouted, "Mr. Steinberg, we're not alone!"

He didn't answer. I called again. Thought I heard a moan.

The dust began to settle. Saw light filtering through it. Then the oddest thing happened. A glowing orb began to appear behind a tall, undamaged building several blocks away. From my perch of torn planks and ceiling plaster, I watched the sun rise over San Francisco.

"Hold on," I yelled through the wall. "Someone's going to help us."

How could another day begin if God had destroyed the world? Wondered if Jesus might come to us again. He could explain Easter to Mr. Steinberg. My head ached. Should have paid more attention in Sunday school.

Noticed a bakery cart on the far side of the street. A horse, still harnessed, was lying on its side, almost buried in bricks. Could only see its hooves and part of its head.

A row of shops and homes across the street leaned to the right as if they'd tipped into one another and somehow kept themselves from going down. The sidewalk in front of them had buckled. Big blocks of cement had been strewn about like tossed pebbles. Water from burst pipes ran down the gutter.

Saw movement on the crooked stairs in front of one of the buildings. Angled my head to match its tilt and watched a family in their nightclothes, all coated hair to toes in gray powder, stagger down the steps. A mother with a toddler tucked under her arm held on to her husband while he gripped the small hand of a little boy, who clutched the hand of an older brother, who had his arm linked through a teenage girl's arm, and she held the elbow of her sister about my age. They looked like a daisy chain of ghosts.

But they'd made it through the worst. They'd gotten out.

Wanted to shout hooray to them, but I choked. Tears streamed down my face.

"Don't move, little girl!" The shirtless man in

suspenders propped a ladder against what remained of the first-story wall and second-floor apartment. The gray father left his family and crossed the street to our side. Figured he must be holding the bottom of the ladder but couldn't see him.

My rescuer climbed to the top rung, then carefully stepped over to what was left of the floor. He crawled over loose bricks and scattered furniture—moving toward me like a cat sneaking up on a bird. Pieces of floorboards gave way under his weight and fell.

He stopped. Dirty lines of sweat streaked his face. "Stay still," he said. "I'll get you out of here." The words were calm, but worry wrinkled his brow.

"I'm okay," I said. "It's Mr. Steinberg. He's over there." I patted the wall. "He's not talking anymore. And my Aunt Sally, she's gone, fell out—"

"All right," he said, beginning his deliberate crawl again. One arm forward, hand grappling for a secure hold. A leg followed. Soon he was within reach.

"Easy now," he said. "Come to me a little at time. Careful." I inched toward him. "Mr. Steinberg?" I said.

"You first," the man said, reaching for me. He put his arm around me and swung me onto his back. "Hold on as tight as you can without strangling me."

He moved backwards with me wrapped around him. The tremors hit again. Felt him slip. The floor jittered. I wrenched my arms off his shoulders and rolled away. Something sharp clipped my chin. Warm ooze trickled.

The man cried out. He slid feet first across the space he'd just crawled as the floor drooped and gave way by the outside edge. I pressed myself next to the wall. All manner of things cascaded to the ground—metal pinged, glass smashed, boards bounced. Squeezed my eyes shut. Prayed the man could hold on to something and not go over. And if he did fall, prayed the father holding the ladder would catch him.

I pushed upright against the wall and moved sideways to the overturned bureau, praying all the while. Then I heard it plainly. A hard thud. And screams as loud as mine.

"Littlebeth!" Mr. Steinberg's cry startled me. I held on to it. He was alive.

"You okay? Your aunt?" he called.

Didn't answer. And couldn't tell him the man who would have saved us was gone too.

"Are you there?" he shouted.

"Yes," I squeaked, my throat too full of dust and tears to get it out proper.

"I smell smoke," he said.

Chapter 12

Splintered wood and plaster slabs shifted beneath my shoes. Took several tries to find a steady place to stand in what remained of the bedroom. Looking out the open space where the outer wall had been, I searched for the fire worrying Mr. Steinberg. Blocks away, plumes of smoke rose in the blue sky.

"I see it!" Made my way back to the landing. Called to him again. Looked for his hand sticking up.

My belly twisted. Small licks of flame appeared on the wall behind the mound that trapped him.

"Is it close?" he called.

"Saw smoke down the street," I said, trying not to lie but afraid to tell him the truth.

Had to find something to span the gap between us. If I couldn't get to him and pull him free of that rubble, he'd burn. I plowed through the debris around me, grabbed and tossed broken boards, frantic for anything I could use as a bridge.

"Gas line ruptured!" Mr. Steinberg shouted, panic in his voice.

Did he feel the heat behind him? I thought of all the broken gas lines, stovepipes, and chimneys in San Francisco. I spun around, desperate now, and then I saw it—the front door. Knocked flat off its hinges, it looked long enough.

Rushing, I stumbled, then caught myself. Moved like a crab the rest of the way. Studying how the door lay on the rug, I figured if I lifted it from the back end, I could walk it up to its full height. Using every muscle, I righted that door, then let it fall forward on top of the loose bricks by the threshold. I shouldered it over the pile with a seesaw motion.

"I'm coming for you." Prayed I could make it over.

"Hurry!"

"Almost there!" With all my might, I pushed the door to the edge of the hole. My heart was pounding so hard, it throbbed in my ears. Sweat slicked my face, stinging the cut on my chin. Moved into position to shove the door across the open space. On my knees, arms stretched across its width, my fingers gripping the door's sides. I drew a powerful breath. Then froze.

It wouldn't work. I wasn't strong enough to hold the full weight of that door all the way over the open space. Gravity would pull the front end of the door down before I could push it all the way to the other side. Pictured it falling through the shaft of the collapsed staircase. Me going down after it.

"Mr. Steinberg, can you sing 'My Bonnie Lies over the Ocean'?"

"What?"

"Helps me to hear you," I said. Mama always sang to settle Joey's fussing. Right now, my nerves needed calming. Figured Mr. Steinberg's did too.

I chanted, "'My Bonnie lies over the ocean'..."

He joined in. "'My Bonnie lies over the sea.' Hurry!"

Singing at the top of my lungs, I looked for a miracle. "'Oh, bring back, bring back'..."

Found a section of wood molding ripped from the ceiling. Long enough and not too heavy, but it felt sturdy. I quickly guided it from my side across to Mr. Steinberg's side. Then I pushed and angled the door onto the molding. It made a perfect rail, bracing the door's weight as I glided it over the open space. A bridge to Mr. Steinberg!

"'...my Bonnie to me'...Can you hear me getting closer?" I crawled, careful to stay in the center of the door. Didn't look down.

When I was across, I scrambled to my feet, then knocked Mr. Steinberg's sideways door over with my heel. Ran into the parlor and recognized the smell of singed hair. Same as my pigtail on Mama's stove top. Burning bits of wallpaper floated in the air. Some landed on Mr. Steinberg's head. I patted them out, then clawed at the bricks pinning him in. Spotted a dustbin on the floor and used it to shovel more bricks. Soon he was able to twist and push, freeing both of his arms. He helped me clear a wider opening then pulled himself up and kicked free of the rubble.

He had on his undershirt, trousers, a boot, and a shoe. Must have jumped into whatever he could grab when the shaking started.

We heard a whoosh. His parlor walls blazed. Mr. Steinberg grabbed my hand. We ran. With no time to crawl, I scurried over the door first, feet practically flying. He followed, crossing it in two long strides.

Cheers and clapping met my ears. Mr. Steinberg and I looked at each other, shocked at the sound, then out to the street where a group of men waved to us.

"Over here! Jump!" one of them shouted.

We moved to the end of the landing near the collapsed staircase. Five men held a canvas tarp stretched tight below us. "It's not far. Jump!"

"Jump or burn," yelled another man.

Mr. Steinberg gripped my arm. "Where's Sally?"

The door-bridge crackled from heat roaring out of his apartment. He shook me. "Where?"

"Outside," I cried. "Gone."

He picked me up and tossed me over the edge. Screaming, flapping my arms, I landed face-first on the taut canvas. A smack so painful, I couldn't breathe for a second. The men relaxed their grip and lowered me onto the ground. Someone pulled me out of the way. I gasped for air and shivered in the morning breeze.

The men re-stretched the canvas to catch Mr. Steinberg. He landed on his backside and swiftly got to his feet.

He shook each man's hand. "You saved our lives," he said.

I looked around for the gray-ghost family but didn't

see them. Thought about the first man who tried to rescue me. Thought about Aunt Sally.

My bones started shaking like winter had me in its grip. Before I knew it, Mr. Steinberg had wrapped me in a blanket. I had no idea where it came from.

"Thank you," he said, hugging me tight. "We're all right now." Took awhile for his warmth and words to stop my trembling.

We stood across the street from our building, watched flames spitting out of the second story. On the ground level, I saw Aunt Sally's shop window had shattered, spewing broken glass over her fine linens and lace. Mr. Steinberg's window held, but his display of hats had been thrown into a jumble.

All sorts of folks were on the street. I'd feared most everyone had disappeared, but so many people hurried by that it made me dizzy.

I turned to ask Mr. Steinberg where they were all going. But he was waving to the men who'd rescued us, wishing them good luck. They headed toward smoke clouds several blocks away. Some people followed them. Most of the others went in different directions.

Mr. Steinberg stared at his shop and shook his head. "It will all be gone soon."

Together, we watched the mixed-up parade moving up and down the street. Some folks were in nightclothes like me; others had put themselves into all the clothes they owned. A man in so many layers of jackets and pairs of pants that he could hardly bend his arms and legs wobble-shuffled down the street, bumped into a boy, then tottered. If he fell, he'd never get back up.

A woman in a coat and hat ran by him, coming toward us. She held a mantel clock out in front of her like a shield. It had stopped at five twelve. Figured that's when the shaking started this morning.

On her heels, a younger woman wearing a crisp, white apron, her hair neatly pinned up, carried an empty birdcage in one hand and a Bible in the other. Her eyes searched this way and that, and her open mouth made no sound.

Baby buggies trundled by us, stuffed with pots, jewelry boxes, framed photos. Where were the babies? A gentleman in evening clothes and a top hat pulled a steamer trunk he'd tied with rope. It scraped along the sidewalk behind him. With a strange grin, he said to everyone he passed, "Save what you can."

I leaned into Mr. Steinberg. "Are you all right?" He was all I had here to care about saving.

"Uh-huh." He rubbed his forehead. "We have to find your aunt. Can't leave without trying." He wiped his eyes.

Wanted to tell him she was likely under a mountain of bricks. The entire wall had given way. Instead, my eyes welled and grief came in heaving sobs. Aunt Sally had confounded me, but she was Papa's sister, just like I was Joey's, and Grandma's daughter. And poor Mr. Steinberg loved her no matter how poorly she treated him.

It hurt to cry so hard. I thought of Aunt Sally's crying spell. Had she been grieving too? For a love she couldn't have? Made my sobbing worse.

Mr. Steinberg used a corner of the blanket, still around my shoulders, to wipe my face, then patted my back.

I longed for Mama's softness, her rose scent, her sweet words in my ear. Wanted Papa to lift me in his strong arms and carry me home. Needed to hear Joey laugh and to taste one of Grandma's pies. Now I wasn't crying for Aunt Sally at all but for me.

Didn't think God would forgive such selfishness. Thought he might tear my aching heart asunder. Wasn't sure what *asunder* meant, but knew it happened when God was angry. Hadn't he torn San Francisco asunder? The man on the corner was telling everyone that he had.

"Repent, the end is here!" The man thumped his chest with his fist. "God destroyed Sodom and Gomorrah; he will destroy us too! Repent, you sinners!"

"I'm sorry." I called to him, almost choking on my tears. "I repent!" Before I could run over to make things right with that corner preacher, Mr. Steinberg grabbed me and turned me to him. The blanket fell.

"This isn't anyone's fault!" His eyes held mine. "It's an act of nature not retribution. That man is crazed with fear."

He held my hand tight and walked me around to the side of our building, where Aunt Sally's bedroom would have been.

"He helps those who help, not those who frighten," Mr. Steinberg muttered, then let go of me as he climbed over the remains of the outer wall.

I tried to keep up but slowed to stare at the skeleton of the building. To see its insides from out here felt wrong. My tears slowed and cooled on my cheeks.

"Stand behind me. And prepare yourself," Mr. Steinberg said as he reached for my hand again. "If I tell you to look away or close your eyes, do it."

I understood. Two years ago I found Grandma's tabby in front of her house, struck by a wagon wheel.

Made me wince to remember. Then I thought of the dead horse lying out there on the street with the bakery wagon.

The debris we searched through had been the safe bedrooms people tucked themselves into last night. I stepped on something, bent to pick it up. One small, white button-up shoe. The kind a little girl might wear with a party frock or an Easter dress. My mind sputtered like a spent fire. Plopping on my fanny, I cradled it like a doll, rocking back and forth.

"Rest here," Mr. Steinberg said, gently taking the shoe from me. He pushed it into his trouser pocket. "Don't move."

I blinked slowly and heavily. Don't know how long I sat there, but a familiar rumble and shaking from below got me to my feet. Powerful jolts sent more bricks tumbling. Mr. Steinberg half carried, half dragged me out of that alley onto the street. The shaking lasted almost as long as the first time.

"Aftershock," he said. "Happens after earthquakes."

Took a minute to catch my breath. I remembered Papa's stories of seeing pond water slosh and trees bend over when he was a boy on the ranch. Couldn't believe I'd just been through an earthquake. Around us, people chattered; some cried. I wondered if there'd ever been one this powerful before.

"Did you find her?" I asked.

Mr. Steinberg coughed and shook his head no.

Smoke filled the sky. Ash floated above us like down feathers after a pillow fight. The gritty air stung my nose and eyes.

The street parade went on and on but faster now. Everyone went in one direction. A man paused long enough to yell, "Get to the Ferry Building!"

From the corner, on the far side of our building, something staggered out of the smoky haze. Mr. Steinberg and I both saw it.

A spirit in a fluttery white gown moved toward us.

Chapter 13

I screamed at the sight of my dead aunt coming for me.

Mr. Steinberg bolted like a racehorse. He caressed her face and wrapped his arms around her. "Dear lady!" he said over and over, kissing her cheek.

I worried the leftover vapor of her departed soul would disappear, and he'd be heartbroken again. She crumpled against him. He carried her to the sidewalk.

"Auntie?" I whispered, tiptoeing near. "Is that really you?"

"Sally, please." Mr. Steinberg patted her hand and tried in vain to revive her. "Don't leave us, not now. Please." He jostled her. "Wake up!"

She lay limp in his arms, only the shallow rise and

fall of her chest giving any hope. Even as thin as she was, I knew he didn't have the strength to carry her far or fast enough to outrun the hungry fire coming our way. We needed help.

The preacher had abandoned his corner pulpit. Ahead, all I saw were backsides of people running. Behind us, a block away, orange flames jumped from rooftop to rooftop. Our building smoldered, but hadn't spread its fire to others.

Terrified we couldn't escape on our own, I searched for anything that could help and then remembered the bakery cart. Saw it on the other side of the street—a small, enclosed wagon with two big wheels. We could unhitch the dead horse and roll down the hill faster than we could run toting Aunt Sally. Might crash, but that was better than burning. I hollered my plan to Mr. Steinberg.

He gently laid Aunt Sally's head down, stood to face the fire raging toward us, and nodded.

We ran to the wagon.

"Won't work," he said, fingering its wood shafts while I unfastened buckles on the leather straps. Flies buzzed around the horse's head. Smoke thickened the air.

"This street goes downhill," I said, talking as quickly

as I could. "Just have to pull the wagon a bit, jump inside, and roll to the sea."

"The shafts will catch and tilt this thing head over end," he said. "We'll break our necks."

"We'll turn it backward, let 'em drag behind," I said.

Mr. Steinberg looked doubtful, but he helped me free the cart from the horse. We strained to lift the shafts and turn the wagon around. He rushed to Aunt Sally, carried her over, and put her inside between baskets of bread.

"Jump in," he said.

"No! You need my help to push it."

"Once it starts rolling down, we won't make it inside," he said.

There wasn't time to tell him I was the fastest kid in Paso Robles. I ran around to the front, which was now the back of the wagon. He lifted one shaft and I picked up the other. We pushed it like a huge wheelbarrow. Heat from the fire warmed our backs and spurred us on.

Didn't have to push long before the wagon gathered speed on its own. Wondered if we should hold on and let the shafts drag us downhill.

Mr. Steinberg yelled, "Drop it!"

We released the shafts and flung ourselves forward,

stretching our arms and legs to chase that horseless, backward wagon. It careened toward the bay. Those wooden shafts scratched the pavement like fingernails on a blackboard. Glancing over my shoulder, I was grateful for the growing distance between us and the inferno.

An explosion sounded, vibrating the ground. I lost my footing and fell down flat on my face. Blood spurted out of my nose.

Mr. Steinberg didn't break his stride. He looked back at me, then ahead to the wagon hurtling downhill with Aunt Sally in it. "Get up, damn it, get up!"

Don't know what shocked me more: the explosion, the blood, or the cursing. I got up. Held my hand under my nose and ran for all I was worth.

As I gasped for breath, I realized this was like my dream before the earthquake. Hadn't been sure who I was trying to catch in that barley field, then that giant was after me. Now *death* was trying to catch me, and I was chasing my only friend, Mr. Steinberg, and he was following a love that kept getting farther and farther away.

"Watch out below!" Mr. Steinberg shouted.

Folks I couldn't see cried out. Their yells, loud and frightened, flew past my ears. That wagon might run over someone the same way Grandma's tabby had been struck and killed. Blood dripped into my mouth. I stopped and spit it out.

If that cart hit someone, it would be my fault, my idea, and my sin.

Started running again. "Watch out!" I called, repeating the warning.

Mr. Steinberg veered right at the bottom of the hill. A few people on the street stared at him, while most everyone else rushed to get out of the burning city.

My lungs ached from the smoke and worry and running so hard. I rounded the same corner as Mr. Steinberg, and there it was. The wagon had jumped the curb and rolled into the side of a building, but not just any building. Large painted letters over the doorway exactly matched the brown printing on the wagon: Perata's Bakery.

I stood there, matted in plaster dust, blood, and ash, so stunned by this homecoming that I forgot everything else. Until my stomach gurgled.

Then I remembered the baskets of bread and climbed into the wagon.

Mr. Steinberg, already inside, held a glazed ceramic jug to Aunt Sally's lips. "Slow, slow," he cooed.

Her eyelashes fluttered as she swallowed. He looked at me. "You're a sight." He didn't add "for sore eyes" like Mama sometimes said.

"What's that?" I asked, looking at the jug. I tore a chunk off a crusty loaf of bread and ate it. The soft inside comforted me.

"Found it under the driver's bench," he said. "Easy." He gave Aunt Sally another sip.

"I'm thirsty too," I said.

"Just wet your whistle, not a full drink. It's red wine." He shifted around to hand me the jug.

Tasted like sour grape juice.

He took the jug back and held it to his own lips.

"What do we do now?" My mouth was full. Didn't care. Stuffed in more bread.

"We give thanks for our lives," he said, closing his eyes for a moment. "And I want to commend you, for your quick thinking and courage." He picked up a loaf and broke off a piece for Aunt Sally, then gave her another sip from the jug.

"Beth?" he asked then paused.

"Like the way that sounds, Mr. Steinberg!" I grinned at him and chewed openmouthed so I could breathe. My nose was stuffy even though the bleeding had stopped.

"Fits you better than Littlebeth," he said. "And you don't seem fond of Elizabeth."

"No, sir. Elizabeth is Grandma's name. Beth is just right for me."

He smiled that friendly way of his—made me want to reach over and hug him.

"Would you tend your aunt while I check the fire's progress?" he asked.

I'd already taken another big bite of bread, so I nodded.

He took a loaf with him. Must have been as starved as me.

"Ben?" Aunt Sally lifted her head and looked for him.

"He'll be right back. Here, take another drink." I held the jug and mimicked him as best I could. "Slowly," I said. Then wondered how Mr. Steinberg would feel, knowing she'd used his first name.

Chapter 14

Mr. Steinberg had been gone too long, and I'd given Aunt Sally too many swigs from the jug to keep her from fretting. It sat empty on her lap. Purple stains splattered the front of her nightgown.

"That accursed Nero has risen again to play his fiddle while *our* city burns, and I for one won't have it." She spoke like an orator, then hiccuped.

Any other time, I'd have had a good laugh about my proper auntie drinking too much wine but not now. There wasn't a chuckle in me. Wanted to go look for Mr. Steinberg but couldn't leave her alone.

I crawled to the end of the wagon and checked outside for him. It was getting hotter. Hoped it was only the sun rising higher. Couldn't see any blue in the sky. I coughed from the gray smoke in the air then scooted back inside the wagon for another bite from my loaf. Wasn't sure how much longer we could wait for Mr. Steinberg before we'd have to flee the fire again.

"Wonder what Grandma would think of Italian bread," I said, offering my aunt a piece. "I love it."

Licked my fingers and used the dampness on them to smooth Aunt Sally's messy hair. It was more frazzled than curly, its luster dulled by the powder of crumbled walls.

"Where's he?" She slurred her words and swatted my hands away.

"Nero?"

"Mr. Steinberg," she said. Another explosion shook the wagon, jangling my nerves. At least the third one I'd counted.

"What *is* that?" I asked.

"Cannon blasts. Are we at war?" Aunt Sally asked.

I was too anxious to stay in that wagon another minute. Aunt Sally was my responsibility now. I had to look around. Check the fire. It was time to decide if we should get moving without Mr. Steinberg.

"Aunt Sally, I'm going outside for that need I'm not

supposed to mention. Be right back." I hopped down before she could stop me.

The street was deserted.

"Hey!" The voice sounded like Mr. Steinberg's, but I couldn't see him through the smoke.

"Beth!"

I ran toward him, tripping when the fourth explosion hit. Didn't fall this time, but my brain pounded inside my head.

"Why are they shooting cannons?" I called, covering my ears.

He came into sight, reached for me, and gave me a quick embrace. "Is your aunt all right?"

"Where were you?" I asked.

"Almost got drafted into a fire brigade." He pulled me toward the wagon.

"She's fuddled from that wine. Jug's empty," I said and shrugged at his startled expression.

"They're dynamiting buildings for fire breaks, but that's causing more fires than it's stopping." He spoke fast. "We have to go."

He crouched beside the wagon and touched a wheel. "Spokes are broken," he said.

"Can we still push it?" I asked.

"No. Safer to walk. We'll go to the Ferry Building and get on a boat out of here." He stuck his head inside the cart and motioned for Aunt Sally to come to him. She crawled until he was within reach and could lift and pull her out.

"She called for you when you were gone," I said as he set her down. "Called you Ben." I raised my eyebrows and smiled.

He ignored me. "Put your arm over my shoulder," he said to Aunt Sally. "I'll help you."

He wrapped his arm around her waist and held the hand she draped over his shoulder.

I looked at them standing so close in the middle of the street in the middle of the day. Only husbands, children, and doctors were supposed to see women in their nightgowns. A scandal anywhere but here—a tumbled-down, burning city.

The nearing fire drew beads of sweat on our foreheads.

"Come on," Mr. Steinberg said. "We have to hurry."

"The bread!" I scampered into the wagon. Seemed wrong to leave it. People, especially escaping people, needed to eat. Lifted the hem of my nightgown to create a sack, then scooped as many loaves into it as I could hold. It made for a lumpy bundle that knocked into my knees with every step.

I recalled how Mama looked when she used her apron to bring fresh vegetables or flowers from her garden to the kitchen—graceful. Not like me.

We'd gone two blocks when I saw bright-blue letters painted on the side of a wooden building: Frank's Freshest Fish.

"Mr. Steinberg, here it is!" The place from the flier I'd found on the train. And where I'd been going the night I met him—where I tried to get Aunt Sally to take me yesterday.

Six crates sat out front, filled with silvery fish laid end to end, several layers deep. They practically sizzled in the heat. The smell and smoke almost made me gag but didn't lessen my excitement.

"I see. Keep moving," he said.

"Golly, if we still had that wine, with this bread, and these fish, it would be like the feast during the Sermon on the Mount when Jesus fed the multitudes," I said, adding, "Maybe we should take some—"

"Maybe we should get out of this city before it kills us," he snapped.

His harsh tone hurt me. We were almost safe now. Why was he mad? Then I realized I'd probably upset him by talking about Jesus and reminding him and

Aunt Sally of their different religions, but I didn't know how to apologize without making it worse. We walked several more blocks in silence.

"Stop. Can't go on." Aunt Sally gasped for air and slipped from Mr. Steinberg's grip. She folded in on herself like a rag doll and went down.

"We're nearly there." Mr. Steinberg tried to lift her but faltered.

"She's tuckered. We all are," I said. "Just a short break."

He sat her on the curb. I leaned against a lamppost.

Mr. Sternberg pointed out the top of the clock tower in front of the Ferry Building.

Ahead, we could see hundreds of people funneling toward it from every intersection.

We'd been on our own for a while. It was a relief to see others. Yet there were so many, and they kept coming. I pulled my upturned nightgown closer to protect the bread.

A loud tooting sounded behind us. I turned to see a horseless carriage rumbling up the road. It weaved around scattered stones and the bumps and dips where the road had lifted and dropped. The driver squeezed his horn at every opportunity. The man wore a plaid cap. His mustache extended beyond his face and blew back in the wind.

I was about to remark on the funny sight to Mr. Steinberg, hoping we could laugh together, but he no longer stood next to me. He'd planted himself in the road, in the vehicle's path. With arms crossed over his head, he waved, signaling the driver to stop.

The machine seemed to slow but still skidded toward Mr. Steinberg. Before a warning left my lips, the automobile hit him. Mr. Steinberg went straight up and landed across the front of the devil's contraption.

Covered my eyes. Bread fell everywhere. Aunt Sally screamed, forcing me to lower my hands and look at her. She tried to stand, but couldn't get off the curb. I rushed to help her.

The noise of screeching tires pained my ears and overpowered the cries of everyone who'd seen the terrible deed. Sprawled facedown over the machine's nose, Mr. Steinberg stayed glued to it as the vehicle stopped.

Aunt Sally and I held on to each other. Silence for a blink of time, then an awful thump when Mr. Steinberg fell onto the road.

Arms linked, we made our way to him. I lowered my aunt to the ground, then dropped to my knees. "Please be alive," I cried, touching his chest. Thought my heart might rip open if he wasn't breathing.

A deep voice bellowed, "Move away!" It was the driver, Satan himself. His big hands grabbed my shoulders and pulled me off Mr. Steinberg.

I thought he wanted to clear the road, to be on his way again.

"You killed him!" I yelled. Rage flowed through me.

He thrust out a large forearm to swipe me away then knelt beside Aunt Sally.

"I'm a doctor," he said to her, as she held Mr. Steinberg's hand. "Let me check him."

Several people paused on the other side of the street, gawked at us, then moved on. No one offered to help. I could hear the roar of the fire marching closer.

The driver pressed his fingers on Mr. Steinberg's wrist. With his mustache and glasses, that devil looked like President Roosevelt. I rubbed my eyes.

"Madam, move aside," he said to Aunt Sally. He put his ear close to Mr. Steinberg's mouth, placed his hands on Mr. Steinberg's head, neck, chest, and legs. A sprinkling of ash already covered his still body. "Your husband is alive. Knocked out, but no worse off than being kicked by a mule, I'd say."

Aunt Sally shook her head and trembled. Her words rattled so fast they tangled into gibberish.

"I'll take him to my hospital." The doctor put a hand under her arm to help her up. "That's where I was going. I'm sorry." His words trailed into a whisper. He cleared his throat, "Help me lift him."

"Can't." She wheezed and clutched her sides.

"Madam?"

Aunt Sally's eyes rolled up, and she fell back. The man caught her.

"She reeks of wine." He looked at me. I nodded.

"Your mother?" He hoisted her into the passenger seat of his vehicle. Her head drooped forward.

"No." I struggled to my feet. "She fell out of her bedroom in the earthquake."

He pointed at Mr. Steinberg, still unconscious on the ground. "Your father?"

Shook my head. Before I could speak or move closer, a flock of people encircled us. "Commandeer that automobile!" a man shouted.

"Take us out of here," another man said.

This skittish herd of folks elbowed me, pushing me back to the sidewalk. I stood on my tiptoes but couldn't see.

"Stop!" The doctor's voice rose above the others.

The only word that mattered, though, was the one he said moments ago: *alive*.

Tried to work my way closer. But there were too many people.

"I have an injured man here!" The doctor's urgent tone silenced them. "Help me lift him."

A woman cried, "We're all going to burn!"

"He has a gun!" a man shouted seconds before the shot fired.

An opening in the crowd appeared. I dashed through it and saw the doctor standing on the running board of his motorcar. He held a pistol high in the air, pointing the barrel heavenward.

"Quiet!" he commanded. "We are not savages." He gestured at two men with his pistol. "Gently put that man into the rear. He's hurt."

The men did as they were told. Mr. Steinberg blinked when they placed him in the vehicle. Oh, what a happy sight. I took a long, deep breath. We'd finally found help.

Most of the folks moved on toward the Ferry Building. Some lingered. The doctor jumped into the driver's seat and honked his horn at the men in front of him. They retreated a few steps.

I hurried toward the machine. A yowling rumble sounded as it came back to life.

"Wait for me!" My words were lost as the automobile sputtered forward, releasing puffs of smoke from its back end.

Stunned for a moment, I stood alone, my heart as flat as the trampled loaves of bread on the road. My legs woke up. I raced after them, waving, shouting.

Thought I might catch up, but even the fastest eleven-year-old is no match for a horseless carriage. The machine turned left, had more power to climb the hill than I did, and shrank in the distance. I saw the motorcar turn once more before it disappeared.

Sparks swirled through the air and fell like red rain in Lucifer's kingdom. I brushed them off, coughed, then spat in the gutter. Felt like bits of the charred city came up from my insides. Wouldn't Grandma and Mama have a fit if they saw me in my sooty nightgown, hacking and spitting in public?

And wouldn't their tongues wag if they knew how much wine my refined auntie drank before being carried off in her nightclothes with Mr. Steinberg? Couldn't muster a smile.

Had to keep moving up the street. Nothing stayed

still for long in San Francisco. The ground had trembled half a dozen times in the last few hours. Aftershocks, explosions, people running from flames—fire lapping up what the earthquake hadn't destroyed, and those firemen blowing up the rest. Behind me was the Pacific Ocean, but there wasn't any water to fight the fire. Nothing made sense.

I looked back downhill at the crowd around the Ferry Building. Its clock tower rose like a beacon of safety. Those same folks who'd surrounded the doctor's automobile had merged into a mob pushing closer and closer to the tower—all of those people trying to escape the city. How would so many find enough boats? I imagined ferries sinking from the weight of the desperate multitudes. Maybe it was better to drown than burn.

Couldn't fathom either choice, so I continued up the street the motorcar had taken. Even though it had made too many turns, gone too far for me to catch, I had to find that doctor's hospital. How could I tell Grandma and Papa I'd lost Aunt Sally in a dying city? And how could I abandon my friend, Mr. Steinberg? I wouldn't let them go. Not like my family had let go of me.

The fire burned several blocks away. Yet, the street I walked up seemed okay. If I didn't count toppled lampposts or twisted slots and rails from the cable cars and trolleys, and ignored the smoke clouds—a new eye-stinging, chest-burning city fog.

A man and woman, each holding a little boy's hand, hurried by me going down the hill. Would Mama and Papa pass a child alone in this disaster without a word of concern or offer of aid? The thought chilled me even though sweat dripped down my back.

I went on, aware of a terrible thirst. The street began to level off. Ahead, I saw an open square with people standing about in small groups, talking, not running, not screaming, not trampling over one another. Calm in the center of chaos. An oasis. Would there be water? My steps quickened. Then the most unexpected thing of all.

A voice I recognized.

Chapter 15

"We must have transport out of this place," demanded a man in booming, accented words. He wore a fine black suit, dusted in ash. His derby, tilted back on his head, revealed thick, ebony hair. A gold nugget stickpin held his tie. It had to be him.

He paced as he spoke. "Find us a wagon," he said to a smaller man standing near stacked trunks and valises. "And guard these from thieves!"

How could that poor fellow do both?

The important man continued to give orders. The voice, the swagger in his step, it could only be him.

"Don Jose!" My voice cracked from dryness. Rushing toward him, I spread my arms.

His dark eyebrows almost flew off his forehead.

"No!" he shouted, holding up an open hand to stop me.

My nose hit the heel of his palm. Blood flowed again, and sparklers went off inside my head. I fell into darkness.

Squinting up at the smoky gray sky, I saw Mr. Caruso's face. His arm was under my neck, supporting me. He held a tin cup to my lips. Water!

Gulping, I hardly noticed I was lying on the ground. Mr. Caruso whispered, "*Piano, piano.*"

Did he want me to play? I didn't know how. Tried to look for a piano in the square, but stringy hair covered my eyes.

"*Piano,*" he said once more.

I put my hand over his to tip the cup. Was too thirsty to think about helping him find a piano.

"Slowly, *bambina, piano.*" His accent turned the words into sweet, rounded sounds.

Piano means slowly I realized then floated on his soft tones. The cup at my lips again brought me back. If I weren't so parched, I'd have slept a month of Sundays in the great Caruso's arms.

"Where are your people?" There was impatience in his voice. Made me think he'd asked the question before. "Gone," I managed to say as a trickle of water escaped the side of my mouth.

"*Poverina.*" The pitiful crease in his brow and the breathy oddness of the word startled me. Had something awful happened? To me?

Struggling to sit upright, I felt his hand curl over my shoulder to hold me steady. I strained to reach for my legs. Still there. I patted my chest, my face, and looked at my hands. Felt my nose. It hurt but had stopped bleeding.

"No, no. No move, child. My valet is getting a constable for you." He nodded at the square.

I pushed hair off my forehead and looked around. Saw the man Mr. Caruso had told to find a wagon. He was talking to a soldier. The soldier had a rifle over his shoulder. He and the valet turned toward me.

"Please, don't let him take me away!" I clutched Mr. Caruso's lapel. The only familiar person I had to hold on to.

"Shh. Is okay." Mr. Caruso motioned the valet and soldier closer, gesturing again as if they weren't moving quickly enough.

Fingering my sore nose, I said, "Think it's broken." Wanted to warn him I'd make a fuss if he tried to hand me over to the soldier. He didn't know how many times my nose had been smacked and bloodied today.

"*Basta.* Enough." Mr. Caruso held me to his chest and rocked me a little. "Shh. Accident, yes? You run into me. Only a bump. A souvenir from Caruso, eh?"

I pulled back but still gripped his jacket. "Don't let that soldier take me. Please! I have to find my Aunt Sally and Mr. Steinberg."

He tried to pry my fingers loose. "The soldier will help you."

"Mr. Steinberg took Aunt Sally and me to see you rehearse yesterday," I said. "Couldn't believe how your voice went so high then low then high again! Didn't understand the words, but the way you sang them gave me gooseflesh. And when Mr. Steinberg told us the story of Don Jose and Carmen, I felt so sorry for you. And Mr. Steinberg too, because he loves my Aunt Sally like you loved Carmen, but Aunt Sally is no Carmen. Now I've lost them."

His jaw dropped.

"I have to find them, Mr. Caruso. They're at a hospital nearby. Don't let the soldier take me." I held on, knuckles clenched tight.

The soldier and valet stared down at us. "Your man here says this is an orphan?"

I leaned against the great tenor.

"No. Is okay. The girl, she will stay with me for now."

"Very generous of you, sir," the soldier said. "We haven't set up anything for displaced children yet."

"*Scusi*, the fire?" Mr. Caruso said. "Are we burning here soon?"

"No, it's not close. We should be safe for the night," the soldier said. "Some members of your troupe are lodging in undamaged homes in the area."

"I think in this town, I will keep away from walls and ceilings!"

"Very good, sir." The soldier turned on his heel and walked off.

Mr. Caruso eased me back so we could see each other. "Okay," he said, "no one will take you away, but sorry, I can no keep you."

I looked at him. Hadn't he just told the soldier I could stay with him?

"My man will give you a biscuit." Mr. Caruso pointed at a cardboard box on top of a trunk. He twitched his finger, directing the valet to open it.

"You must find a neighbor or friend, understand? Someone near your home who knows you." He rose to one knee, then groaned a little as he stood upright. Brushing his trouser legs with his hands, he smiled at me.

"You know opera? Hear it before yesterday?" he asked.

I shook my head no. The valet handed me a cookie. I'd expected a buttermilk biscuit like Grandma's, not a large sugar cookie. Thought of Grandma's luscious prizewinners—crisp on the outside, chewy on the inside—pieces of Heaven, Papa always said. My mouth watered.

"Well, you start with the best, no?" Mr. Caruso patted his chest and released a booming laugh.

Wondered if Grandma would tell him how rude it was to brag. Or if she'd excuse his boasting because he *was* the greatest tenor in the world.

"I want to go home." It slipped out, surprising me like the cookie.

"*Sì*, good. My man will walk with you." He grinned at me. "*Buona fortuna.*"

I didn't move.

"Another biscuit," he said to his valet as he waved his hand at the box of cookies then jabbed his thumb in my direction. His smile shrank by half.

"Ciao. Bye, bye." Mr. Caruso dipped his chin at me and cleared his famous throat.

I didn't speak.

"Ciao," he said again, shooing me with a flick of both hands.

I stared at him.

"Give her a dollar!" he told his valet.

"Mr. Caruso, you're the only one I know here. Please help me."

Waves rolled underneath us as if the earth had become the ocean. We swayed, unsteady. Heard gasps and cries around the square. Mr. Caruso's eyes stretched wide.

I wanted to say it was only an aftershock to calm him, but his fearful gaze seemed focused on something so far away that it stopped me. I wondered if he was feeling the suffering of his own people in Naples.

Chapter 16

Dark smoke plumes curdled in the sky. We sat on trunks arranged like chairs in a parlor, even though we were on the sidewalk across from the square. Told Mr. Caruso and his valet about my family sending me to San Francisco two days ago and described everything that had happened since the earthquake.

Took a breath and said, "Aunt Sally and Mr. Steinberg are going to be fearful worried about me out here by myself. I have to find them."

The valet picked up the box of cookies and put it on my lap. Mr. Caruso held a white handkerchief embroidered with E. C. to his forehead. He dabbed his brow. None of us spoke for a while. Figured Mr.

Caruso needed time to put my English words into his Italian ones.

At last he sighed, coughed, and said, "We will help you."

He spoke quickly in his language to the valet. Then he took the cookie box from me and handed it back to his man. Mr. Caruso walked me over to the fountain in the square. He soaked his handkerchief in the water, squeezed it, and wiped my forehead and cheeks. He was careful to be gentle near my nose and on my chin. I'd forgotten about the cut there until it stung when he touched it.

His clean hankie darkened with the soot and dried blood he removed.

"So you are a girl under all this!" Mr. Caruso rinsed the cloth again, then wiped around my eyes.

I winced.

"Oh, this does not come off. You have the black eyes like a prizefighter, no?" He wet the handkerchief and hung it over the rim of the fountain. "They will heal. Is not bad."

He smiled at me. "*Bellissima!*"

Knew the word meant something good, because he looked at me in a kind way. My heart filled. But it was such an odd feeling—almost happy—that my bones softened, letting in the jitters.

Mr. Caruso hugged me until I stopped shivering. He whispered musical words, trilling vowels together. He pressed the damp hankie on my forehead once more.

His valet rushed over holding up two fingers and talking a blue streak in Italian. I picked out what sounded like *hospital.* There must be two near here. He pointed at a teenage boy, who stood by the trunks. Mr. Caruso handed his man some money to pay the boy to guard his things. The valet returned with the box of cookies, a sketch pad, and some pencils. Mr. Caruso tucked the pencils into a pocket and the pad under his arm. I carried the cookies. The valet led the way.

"We are ready for an adventure, no?" asked Mr. Caruso, walking beside me.

I'd already had too many adventures today. Just wanted to get to the hospital. Hoped we'd soon find Aunt Sally and Mr. Steinberg. Didn't know how long my legs could carry me, but I'd crawl if I had to. Prayed they'd be all right. And that if Mama and Papa had heard news of the earthquake, they wouldn't worry too much about me. But maybe enough so they'd want me back and would never, ever send me away again. The last part felt wrong, even though I meant it, so I asked forgiveness to be on the safe side and added a big thank-you for leading me to Mr. Caruso.

A few blocks up the hill, the great man had already eaten four cookies. There were only three left. I held the box tight.

"How far do we have to go?" I asked the valet.

He shrugged and motioned for Mr. Caruso and me to keep up. Strange that the servant was now our leader.

I put my hand into Mr. Caruso's. "Are you still hungry?"

He smiled and squeezed my hand, but before he could answer, we heard a terrible noise. Screeching whines and pounding. Sounded like a horse throwing a fit. My tummy churned. Figured the poor animal must be trapped, but I kept walking.

A few paces ahead, the valet stopped. "There!" He pointed to a side street and took off running.

"Come back," I called. "We don't have time."

"Maybe is transport for us, no?" Mr. Caruso said. "Will help us get to hospital."

"Drat, blast it!" I shoved the cookie box at him, then ran after the valet. That little fella needed help. He probably didn't know anything about horses, being a gentleman's man.

The cries and stomping grew louder as I passed broken crates of vegetables and overturned barrels in front of a building marked Warehouse and Delivery. Next to it was a stable, its door wide open. No people around.

From inside I heard fierce kicking and snorting, and then I made out soft words from the valet. At the rear of the stable, the small man faced a battered stall and tried to sweet-talk a panicked horse towering over him. The animal thrust its chest against the short door, turned, and kicked its hind legs into the side wall, splintering it and crying all the while.

If the horse broke free, it would trample the valet. It was that scared of the smell of smoke and the shaking and being trapped alone. No other horses were here. Wondered when the horse last had food or water.

The valet's gentle words became firm commands, but they didn't work. The horse was frantic. Just then, Mr. Caruso walked through the door carrying the cookie box like a tray.

"Sing," I called to him. "Sing your opera!"

He looked at me for a few seconds then at his valet, who gestured for him to try it.

Mr. Caruso set the box on the ground, stood tall, breathed in, and released the most famous, powerful voice in the world. His perfect notes bounced off the boards of the stable walls. He sang the same song that had taken my breath away and prickled my skin yesterday.

The horse whinnied, twisted its neck, and strained to see the source of the amazing sound. It clomped one hoof then the other and shook its head, casting off a wide spray of sweat. The valet jumped back.

Mr. Caruso sang on. The horse's breathing steadied. It stood motionless, dumbstruck. Another audience won over.

I went to the valet. "Use your jacket to cover its eyes."

"*Sì*, good." He slipped off his coat, then slowly climbed onto the stall door and reached over to pat the animal.

Mr. Caruso kept singing. The horse listened and stayed calm while the valet wrapped his jacket around its head and tied the sleeves under its neck to use for a lead.

I was ready to get back on our way and turned to tell the great tenor he could stop his song when I saw her. A little girl crouched behind a bale of hay on the other side of the stable.

Her small hands covered her head. She wore a shiny blue tunic and dark pants, different from any clothes I'd ever seen. Long black hair traced the curve of her back.

I took the same care going to the girl as the valet had with the horse. "Hello," I said softly. "Don't be afraid."

When I touched her shoulder, she stiffened and whimpered in the strangest gibberish. Stranger than Mr. Caruso's language.

"It's okay. We won't hurt you," I said.

Slowly, she looked up at me with narrow, dark eyes. I'd only seen people from the Orient in pictures, but I knew many Chinese came to California for jobs because my family talked about them.

Grandma said Chinamen smoked opium and ate dogs. Papa said they worked hard, that we wouldn't have the railroad without them. Papa always looks for the good in people. Grandma sees the worst. Especially in me.

The little girl in the stable was as scared as everyone else in this city. Couldn't imagine her smoking because she was younger than me, but I guessed most people, even Grandma, would eat whatever they could if they were hungry enough.

Told the girl she was safe with us. Didn't seem like she understood a thing I said.

"Beth." I pointed at myself. First time I'd said the name Mr. Steinberg called me. "I'm Beth." Repeated it, then put my finger on her chest. "Who are you?"

The girl pressed against my legs, trembling.

I gently lifted her arms until she stood beside me, just half my size. Wanted to introduce her to the men. Saw them in the far corner, near the entrance with the horse, and—I blinked, not trusting my eyes—a wagon! It was pushed back against the wall alongside hay bales, the tack, and tools.

Was so focused on the frightened horse, I'd missed it. But Mr. Caruso hadn't.

Holding the girl's hand, I said, "Everything's fine now. You're okay." We walked toward the wagon. I stopped at the cardboard box, still on the ground. Picked it up, opened it, and took out a piece of crumbled cookie. I put it close to my mouth, pretended to chew, then handed it to her. She understood, ate it, held out her hand for more. I gave her another piece.

"Su Ling," she said, pointing at herself.

We smiled at each other.

Mr. Caruso sat on a bale of hay watching his valet hitch the horse to the small wagon. He heard me walking over and said, "We have trans—" He stopped mid-word. Stared at me and Su Ling.

I told the men how I'd found her hiding. "We can look for Su Ling's people after we find mine," I said, offering the open box of cookies to Mr. Caruso.

He shook his head no. "First we get my things, then we go to hospital."

I went to the valet with the box. He paused, took a few pieces, then continued harnessing the animal, a servant again, no longer our leader. The horse seemed happy to be doing something familiar. I held the box up to its mouth so it could lick the cardboard clean.

"Tell me where the hospital is," I said to the valet. "I'll walk there with Su Ling while you go back to the square."

"No, *cara,*" Mr. Caruso said as he stood, brushing hay off his trousers. "Is better to stay together, for safety."

Almost argued with him but held my tongue. The valet lifted Su Ling up to the wagon and helped me climb in. He winked at me. Figured he knew what I wanted to say. Had no choice, though, but to trust him and his boss. Didn't know where to go without them.

Chapter 17

I offered to drive the wagon since both men were city folk and might not know how. The valet said no. He held the reins and snapped them like an expert. That man was as talented in the real world as Mr. Caruso on the opera stage. I sat between the two of them. Su Ling perched atop the famous tenor's lap.

"Now we see if that boy has protected or stolen my belongings," Mr. Caruso said.

I almost begged to go to the hospital first but thought better of it. The great man had agreed to help me. I needed to be careful of his feelings—even though he was only anxious about things, while my injured aunt and friend needed me. Couldn't risk making Mr. Caruso angry and have him change his mind.

When we returned to the square, I put my hand on the tenor's arm. "Let's stay in the wagon." Feared he might wander off. Didn't want to lose any more time. "Your valet can take care of the baggage."

Mr. Caruso looked at me as if he might be reconsidering his promise to help, but he remained seated. A man of his word after all, or maybe it was just that Su Ling had fallen asleep in his arms.

The young fellow who'd guarded the valises and trunks helped the valet put them in the wagon. Couldn't see the position of the sun with so much smoke in the sky. But figured it must be well past noon by now. If we needed to check more than one hospital, we'd better hurry.

Almost jumped down to help load but decided it was best to stay near Mr. Caruso. Something caught my eye. The square had changed since we'd been gone. The air was smokier and there were more soldiers. A woman ordered one of them to get her a meal. He ignored her. She cursed then pushed him. He arrested her.

"At least he'll have to feed me," she called over her shoulder as he led her away.

Mr. Caruso shook his head, said some Italian words.

Maybe he was saying how folks were getting tired of being scared and hungry. I was worn out from hunger and running scared. Looked like Su Ling was too. Wished I could sleep and eat, but had to keep us moving, had to find my aunt and friend.

Thought about how wild our horse had been while trapped inside that stable smelling smoke. I feared what would happen to people if the fires weren't put out soon.

The valet hopped into the back of the wagon and opened a leather case. He unpacked four clean handkerchiefs, took them to the fountain, wet them, and returned to show us how to fold the hankies into triangles and tie them around faces. We looked like outlaws—members of Jesse James's gang about to rob a bank. But those damp masks helped filter the smoke we breathed. Thought how lucky Mr. Caruso was to have such a handy man taking care of him. Lucky for me and Su Ling too.

Soon we were heading back up the same hill that we'd just walked. The valet turned a few blocks past the lane with the stable, then went several more blocks before going up another hill. On one side of the street stood fine houses, untouched by the earthquake, while just across from them were homes with tilted roofs, twisted porches, and broken windows. Drew a big breath at the sight and sucked that hankie triangle into my mouth. Had to huff it out.

Su Ling giggled. She inhaled her mask then loudly blew, imitating me. The valet and Mr. Caruso did the same. Silliness felt like a tonic, and we all laughed in the same language. Until a thunderous *boom, boom, boom* almost jolted us off the wagon bench.

The horse skittered. Mr. Caruso clutched Su Ling to his chest. His valet pulled the reins taut and held the horse steady.

"They're blowing up more buildings," I said.

We turned around to see the city being swallowed by crimson flames, smoke billowing above it.

The valet clicked his tongue. We moved on in silence.

Mr. Caruso shifted Su Ling on his lap and said, "What's this?" He put his finger under a string around her neck and lifted it. The string was attached to a card that had been hidden under her tunic.

"Let me see," I said. There were strange markings on it.

The valet looked over. "Chinese writing," he said. "An address perhaps?"

I held the card, still connected to the string around Su Ling's neck. "Was she being sent somewhere like a package? Like a crate of those vegetables near the stable?"

"It's possible she came from a ship," said the valet. "The docks are not far from the stable."

"Hospital!" Mr. Caruso pointed to the top of the hill. Built of stone, the hospital looked like a castle fortress from olden times.

My heart quickened. I dropped the card and tugged his sleeve. "You'll wait for me, won't you, while I look for my aunt and Mr. Steinberg?"

"*Sì*, if does not take too long," he said.

A large, grassy lawn in front of the building held hundreds of people. Some were talking in groups; others stood in lines. A few hurried around the grounds as if on urgent missions. As we traveled closer, I saw the injured lying on cots outside—long rows of them—and heard their moans and cries. Looked as though we'd come upon a terrible battlefield after the fighting had ended.

The valet pulled the wagon up the curved path to the hospital's entrance. I tried to see the faces of the people on the cots, but my eyes stopped at the blood-soaked clothes, the limbs sticking out at impossible angles, the burned and blistered flesh. I turned away from the misery. Took a breath, drew in the mask, then forced myself to look once more.

A man in a stained white coat moved from one person to the next. A doctor, I reckoned, but not the one who'd taken Aunt Sally and Mr. Steinberg away in his horseless carriage. I would never forget that man's face.

Several women in dirty aprons tended the wounded. Their shoulders sagged like they were tired. Wondered how long they'd been taking care of these people.

"Are they all afraid to be inside?" I asked Mr. Caruso.

"Perhaps. Or there are too many," he said, climbing down from the wagon.

He offered his hand to steady me as I jumped to the ground. Su Ling waited for Mr. Caruso to open his arms to her and half leaned, half fell into them.

"Okay," he said, setting her down. The three of us pulled our masks from our faces. It was easier to breathe on the hill.

Mr. Caruso told his valet to move the wagon away from the entrance to a field nearby. Then he gestured at Su Ling and said to me, "This one, you watch."

She seemed to understand and clutched my hand with both of hers.

Mr. Caruso approached a nurse. "Madam?"

She swung around, her lips pressed into a straight line. She looked down at Su Ling.

"Whites only," she said.

"Please," I said, "I'm looking for my aunt."

Her mouth drooped into a frown.

"My aunt is white, and so am I, and so is Mr. Caruso, and if you look at Su Ling's skin, it's the same as yours, covered in soot."

Mr. Caruso pulled me behind him. Su Ling followed, still holding my hand.

"Madam, this day has been difficult for you. For all of us. But please, this child is alone until we find her family."

The nurse didn't change her expression but nodded at me. I explained about the doctor and horseless carriage. She told us to stand in line with the others looking for loved ones.

First, I went up and down each row of cots, looking at every face then I followed Mr. Caruso to a table where two men sat with stacks of papers in front of them.

A line of folks waited their turn to check the list of names on those papers. Next to the table sat four boxes overflowing with items like dolls, hats, shawls, and trinkets. Possessions someone might recognize from a person they knew who'd been brought here.

"This takes too much time. Tell them who I am." Mr. Caruso shifted from one foot to the other.

His haughty tone bothered me. Being famous didn't make him better than these folks.

"Everyone here is someone," I said. "They're all looking for people like we are."

I realized he didn't care about who I was trying to find. He was only doing a lost girl a favor. Thought he was too important to wait in line.

He grumbled. "You have found patience, no? *Brava.* But why should it take all of us to stand here? I will go to the wagon."

I locked my gaze on him, willed him to stay. I feared he might think he'd done his favor by bringing me here, then leave with his valet and wagon. How would I get to the next hospital if Aunt Sally and Mr. Steinberg weren't here? Su Ling looked at me then Mr. Caruso and back to me.

The ground trembled. A deep roar rumbled up as the earth jerked back and forth. I held on to Su Ling. Mr. Caruso drew us both close. We fought to keep our balance. Some people dropped to their knees. Then the aftershock stopped.

No one left the line. Not even the great tenor.

"Worse one in a while," a woman in front of us said.

When my turn came, the man at the table flipped

pages. No Morgans or Steinbergs. "Sorry," he said. "Try the boxes."

I shifted through one box, then another. Su Ling tried to help but didn't know what I was doing and got in the way. "No!" My tone pushed her back. Patting her arm, I smiled an apology.

Already felt awful about rummaging through other people's things. And now I'd hurt Su Ling's feelings. But I was desperate for any clue, so I kept searching. Dropped a pocket watch, picked up a brooch. Realized then that neither Aunt Sally in her nightgown, nor Mr. Steinberg in his undershirt and trousers, had anything with them that could have been collected.

Mr. Caruso cleared his throat and made other annoying sounds. Su Ling whimpered. Someone brought a lantern to the table as daylight started to fade.

When I pulled my hand from the last box, it brushed against the leather of a small shoe, my thumb rubbing its buttons. I held up the girl's shoe I'd found behind our building this morning. The one Mr. Steinberg put in his pocket. I'd forgotten about it.

Felt Mr. Caruso's hand on my back. "Is something?" he asked.

Cradling the shoe, I told him about it.

"So he is here!" Mr. Caruso said.

"It might mean he's…" Couldn't say the word I feared, but I knew most of the things in these boxes belonged to people who couldn't claim them because they were gone. They would only be keepsakes for their families.

"Doesn't mean anything," I said, tossing it back into the box.

Mr. Caruso retrieved the shoe.

"Come," he said.

He walked us back to the cots. Avoiding the nurse we'd talked to, he found the doctor we'd seen when we arrived and handed him the shoe. "Describe your people," Mr. Caruso said to me.

When I finished telling the doctor my story, he sighed, pushed his glasses up his nose, and looked at me.

"Yes, I remember your aunt and the gentleman." He gave the shoe back to Mr. Caruso.

Thought I'd burst out of my skin. "Where are they?" I turned in a circle, scanning those cots again. How could I have missed them?

He pulled a pad from his pocket and began writing.

"My colleague brought them here, as you said, but we sent your aunt, along with other seriously injured women, to the Southern Pacific Hospital. Heard the railroad had opened it to the public after the earthquake. Their facility wasn't as damaged as ours."

He tore off a piece of paper and handed it to Mr. Caruso. "That's the address."

"Where's the gentleman?" I asked, practically jumping up and down.

"Oh, he only had some broken ribs. I wrapped his chest. He didn't want to stay here. Said he had to find someone." The doctor paused. "You, maybe?"

"Let's go." I pulled Mr. Caruso's jacket.

The doctor said, "You'll have to wait until morning. There's a dusk-to-dawn curfew. Talk of looters and martial law."

Mr. Caruso walked us past the lawn to look for the wagon. He assured me we'd go to the other hospital first thing tomorrow, but now we needed to eat, to rest. I tried to listen, but his words stuck together like gobs of mud. All I could think about was Mr. Steinberg wandering out there through the fire and ruins, searching for me.

When we found the wagon, it stood alone, without the horse or valet. We'd been gone a long while. Mr. Caruso wrapped his knuckles on the sideboards and whistled. The valet called to us. Seconds later his silhouette appeared. The horse walked slowly behind him. He must have taken it to graze in the field on the other side of the hill.

After he tied the animal to the back of the wagon, the valet pulled out blankets from a trunk and spread them on the ground. Then he set out a fancy tin box of chocolates and a canteen. We devoured all the candy and drank the water in a few minutes.

Mr. Caruso thanked his man for reviving us. He opened his sketch pad, looked around, then started drawing. Su Ling curled up next to me and was already fast asleep. The valet found enough moisture in the bottom of the canteen to sprinkle our masks for the night.

I pulled Su Ling's hankie up to cover her nose. Before I lifted my own, I asked Mr. Caruso if he had children.

"*Sì*. Little boys," he said, working his pencil over the paper. "In Italy with their mama." He looked up. His eyes glistened in the orangey glow from the fires consuming the city below.

"In Naples? Where that volcano erupted?" I'd been too worried about my own troubles to think much about his country's woes or that he might have family in danger.

"No, *cara*. They are fine. Yet, I must return to them. Tomorrow. Understand?"

"But after we go to the next hospital?"

"*Sì. Sì*," he said, and went back to sketching.

I looked over at the valet, wanting him to agree, but he was lying down with his mask up, asleep or pretending to be.

Mr. Caruso put his pad down. He pulled a photograph from the inside pocket of his jacket and handed it to me. "You know this man?"

I held it close. "President Roosevelt! And he signed it for you."

The tenor had Bully-Boy Teddy next to his heart. It pleased him that I recognized how special that picture was.

"This is my passport," he said, "to the Oakland ferry and the train to New York and a ship home." He carefully tucked the photograph back into his jacket.

Told him how much Papa admired our president. How impressed he'd be to hear I'd met someone who actually knew him. Told him about Joey and Mama then asked if they had apple pie in Italy, because even if they did, he'd never eaten anything as good as Grandma's pie.

He pulled up his mask, motioning for me to do the same and to go to sleep. It might have been like a regular campout if the firelight wasn't an entire city burning and if we'd been able to see stars in the smoke-choked heavens. I closed my eyes and tried to dream of home.

Daylight. Dew in my hair. Screams.

The shrieking woke me.

Chapter 18

Thursday, April 19, 1906

"It's a-coming, it's a-coming!" a woman hollered.

I sat up fast, searched for the fire but didn't see flames. Couldn't tell who was yelling. Su Ling covered her ears and snuggled beside me. Mr. Caruso groaned, squeezed his eyes shut, and shook his head, flapping thick, black hair over his brow and temples.

Sounded like the lady's shouts came from the closest end of the lawn. Before I could get to my feet for a better look, the valet appeared gripping the handles of three metal cups in one hand and holding a plate of bread slices and beans in the other. He smiled as if nothing was out of sorts.

He must have been up early to stand in line for food.

After giving us each a cup and setting the plate on our ash-coated blanket, he pointed toward the noise and pretended to rock a baby in his arms.

"Soon it will be born," he said.

Mr. Caruso clinked his cup to mine. "To the new *bambino*," he said, almost sipping the warm tea through his mask.

Su Ling and I pulled our hankies down, but before we could take a sip or bite, Mr. Caruso sopped up more than half the beans with the biggest piece of bread.

During breakfast, the woman's screams had us all wincing. Didn't know birthing babies was such a loud job. Wondered if Mama sounded like...No...Couldn't think about me or Joey causing Mama pain...Pushed that thought from my mind, quick.

The valet hitched the horse to the wagon as fast as he could. That poor woman's yowls had us scurrying to be on our way. And I blessed her for that, because we needed to find my aunt, and hopefully Mr. Steinberg too, before Mr. Caruso used his passport to travel home.

Settled in the wagon, the four of us put on our freshly dampened masks. The smoke and falling ashes were worse than yesterday. I looked toward the lawn. The screaming had stopped. Couldn't see through the huddle of people gathered nearby. Then we heard the baby's cry.

"*Buona fortuna,*" both men said at the same time.

Hard to believe new life could come into a destroyed city. Maybe it was a good sign.

"Let's go," I said.

The valet flicked the reins.

"Today I am—" Mr. Caruso coughed and had to spit over the side of the wagon. "I am getting the hell out of this town."

A layer of black floated overhead like the brim of a gentleman's top hat, like the ones Mr. Steinberg sold in his shop.

"Hurry," I said as we headed down the hill.

Block after block, I searched for Mr. Steinberg. He was out here alone. I didn't know if he had the strength to get very far. Feared for him.

"How much longer to the other hospital?" I asked.

Mr. Caruso shrugged. He pulled a pencil from his pocket, took his sketch pad out from under the bench, and opened it. He stroked his pencil quickly across the page, made sharp lines and curves, then turned the tip of the pencil on its side to shade in sections of his drawing.

Su Ling, wedged between me and Mr. Caruso, poked my leg to get me to look at his picture—a bleak scene of rubble and ruin—but I only wanted to look for Mr. Steinberg.

The farther we drove, the more debris littered the streets. In some places, the road had been ripped open, making it impassable. We had to backtrack to another street and work our way over. Sections of sidewalk had been raised by the earthquake, then tossed into craggy mounds. Bricks and timber, shaken loose from buildings, were strewn across our path. Navigating these obstacles made our journey slow.

I couldn't stop fidgeting, which irritated Mr. Caruso to no end. Volunteered to jump out and clear the way to speed things up, but the valet swatted me back. He gestured for Su Ling and me to climb behind them and sit low in the back of the wagon.

"But then I can't look for Mr. Steinberg," I said. "You won't recognize him."

Mr. Caruso thrust his finger at me and wagged it. "No safe now."

In the distance, flames rose like red gushers, spewing white-hot embers that ignited whatever they touched. To our right stretched a landscape dotted with charred remains. Wondered about my aunt's neighborhood. Were the shops and apartments and Maria's Cantina all gone now?

I slunk to the wagon's floor, pulling Su Ling with me. I called Mr. Steinberg's name every few minutes. In between, I prayed for Aunt Sally. Wanted to find my friend and take him to her.

Mr. Caruso nudged me with the canteen, making motions to sip, then to sprinkle more water on our masks. I stood to pass it back to him. Saw a soldier holding his hand up for us to stop.

"Where you headed?" The soldier's voice was thick and dry, like the smoky air surrounding us.

"Railroad Hospital first, ferry to Oakland next," Mr. Caruso said.

I leaned over the side of the wagon. "We're looking for a skinny fellow with dark hair and brown eyes, named Ben Steinberg."

"Haven't seen him." The soldier walked up to me, peered over the wagon's side, and stared at Su Ling, who had scrunched herself into a ball.

"That hospital's evacuating patients from the fire. Better get there quick if you're looking for someone," he said and then added, "They might need your wagon."

Mr. Caruso and his man chattered in their language, talking over each other. Su Ling reached for me and tried to say my name, but it came out like a *baa* from a lamb. I cuddled her and felt her damp forehead.

It was plain the men were worried about the wagon, but I had to get to my aunt.

"Papa and Grandma won't ever forgive me if I don't find their Sally," I said.

Mr. Caruso put his hand on my shoulder. Sweat rolled off his face. Near the fires, it felt hotter than August. "We stop the wagon before the hospital," he said. "You and me, we go to find your aunt." He pointed at his valet. "Then, we go to Oakland."

"Su Ling?" I gripped her hand.

"*Va bene.* Okay. She comes to find your aunt too."

Was going to ask about helping to find her people. But figured I'd have to do that on my own. Didn't think Mr. Caruso had any more favors in him.

We heard a deafening blast a block over. My ears rang. The horse reared, shook its head, and fought the reins. The valet struggled to pull the straps tight and hold on. His muscles strained against the startled animal's power. The wagon swerved as the horse twisted one way, then the other. The horse's panic grew with a second explosion. Our wagon would be smashed to smithereens if the horse ran wild on streets covered in rubble.

Mr. Caruso started singing: "'In the good old

summertime, strolling through the shady lanes, with your baby mine.'"

The magnificent sound stunned the animal into being calm like it had yesterday at the stable. Think I was as surprised as the horse to hear the famous tenor croon a modern tune. We'd sung "In the Good Old Summertime" on our family campout. It was Papa's favorite.

The valet gently maneuvered the wagon down a large street and then turned up a side alley just before we reached the hospital. We could see flames rising blocks away, but the fire hadn't turned this direction yet.

The soldier had been right about the evacuation. Automobiles, carts, and wagons were lined up in front of the building. Nurses rushed about, pointing here and there, holding papers. Hoped my aunt's name was on one of those papers.

It bothered me that Mr. Caruso wanted to hide the wagon with his trunks and bags so he could use it for himself instead of helping to take people from the hospital to a safer place. Wasn't even his wagon. Just because he could sing opera better than anyone else didn't mean he shouldn't do his part.

But he had, I told myself. The famous tenor *was* helping me. Couldn't forget that. Helping, even though he wanted to go home to his own family.

Mr. Caruso climbed down. Su Ling and I followed. The valet stayed on the bench. He'd wrapped the leather reins around his hands to be ready for the next blast or shake. Su Ling's tight grip hurt my knuckles. I didn't complain because my latch on Mr. Caruso was even stronger, and he held up to it. We walked around the corner into a jabber-jangle of people yelling orders from the top steps of the hospital's entrance. Folks on the sidewalk shouted back questions. Horseless carriages sputtered and rumbled while actual horses snorted and clopped their hooves as they pulled carts and buck-boards forward to meet the stretchers being carried out of the building.

A clanging bell overhead stopped everyone's move-ment like they were playing a game of statues. Whether people were on the steps or the street or in automobiles or wagons, each one held the same pose, staring up at the roof.

A man leaned over the edge, a long-handled bell in his hand. He shouted, "Fire's jumped to the Emporium. Wind's blowing this way!"

The man didn't have to ring that bell again to un-freeze the statues. Folks knew they had to move faster than those hot embers blowing toward us. In the haze of smoke, the race to haul patients out of the hospital had the look of a quick-paced kinetoscope. But this wasn't a moving picture with a pretend villain chasing a damsel. There might not be a hero or a happy ending.

Mr. Caruso remained a statue. I yanked his hand. He didn't move.

I strained to see the faces on the stretchers carried past us. Asked a nurse if my auntie was on her list, but she ignored me and climbed into the back of a cart.

"Have to go inside," I said, pulling Mr. Caruso toward the first step.

"No." He wrenched his hand free of mine. "The fire," he said, "it will overtake us. We go now."

Su Ling let loose a string of strange squeaks and broke away from me. Mr. Caruso and I watched her run up the steps. "Come on," I said to him.

He shook his head. "I wait five minutes." He held up his open hand and wiggled his fingers, then closed them into a fist. "Five." He jabbed his thumb toward the alley where the valet waited. "No more."

I followed Su Ling. She'd gone past a pair of men who had linked their arms to make a seat for an old man in a robe. They toted him out of the hospital like they were carrying a pharaoh from Egypt.

Looking back, I saw Mr. Caruso standing still while others rushed around him. "Thank you!" I called in case I didn't see him again.

Found Su Ling inside the lobby with a young woman from her own side of the world. The lady wasn't dressed like Su Ling though. She had on the same kind of skirt and blouse as Mama or Aunt Sally might wear. She listened to the sounds flowing from Su Ling and nodded.

"Ma'am," I said, talking over the strange words, "is Sally Morgan here?"

The way she looked at me, I worried she didn't understand or thought I was a robber in my mask. Mr. Caruso's warning echoed in my mind. How many minutes left?

"Please!"

"Could be a few patients on the second floor still to be moved," she said as plain as any American.

Took the stairs, two at a time. I shouted back, "Don't take Su Ling. Wait for me!" Imagined a stopwatch. A minute to find Aunt Sally, another to get back to Su Ling, another to reach the hidden wagon—fastest kid in Paso Robles—I could do it.

Run.

Run.

I slid around a corner, darted between empty beds, leaped over a pair of abandoned crutches. Never slowed until I saw the auburn-colored mane fanned out across a white pillow.

Aunt Sally! My chest heaved, I pulled down my hankie to call out but then I saw him. Mr. Steinberg was sitting on the side of her bed, holding her hand, leaning close, and whispering to her.

Mr. Steinberg and Aunt Sally.

Together.

Alive.

Like a curtain, my auntie's hair separated me from them—protected their privacy. Somehow Mr. Steinberg had traveled through the mangled streets and peril to find her.

With their city knocked down and burning, maybe old rules didn't matter. Maybe they could be sweethearts now. If a baby could be born in such a devastated place, anything was possible.

Except stopping time.

I sighed. Five minutes had already passed. Mr. Caruso and his valet were on their way to Oakland. Su Ling was probably gone too. But my aunt and friend were here, holding hands.

Mr. Steinberg looked up.

"Beth!" His voice lassoed me out of my thoughts. "Beth!" He stood.

A man carrying a woman to the stairs yelled, "You're on your own. Get out now!"

Aunt Sally turned over and opened her arms.

I ran to her.

Chapter 19

"Fire's here," I said it softly. Figured we were the last ones in the hospital.

Flames crackled outside. Three beds away, heat blistered the wall. Paint bubbled. Thought I heard each bulge sizzle then pop.

Windowpanes burst in the heat. Glass flew. I ducked. Yellow fingers reached inside, touched the curtains, set them ablaze.

"Can't lift her!" Mr. Steinberg said. He reached for me. I saw the bandages around his middle. Broken ribs, the doctor had said.

Dark smoke crept across the ceiling toward us.

Aunt Sally looked at me with a swollen face I barely

recognized.

"Take his hand," she said. "Run!"

Her words pinched my heart.

She loved him the same way he loved her. And she wanted him—and me—to live. No matter what happened to her.

Before another thought entered my head, I tugged the sheet beneath her away from the mattress. Mr. Steinberg understood. He pulled out his side and held it up, using his long arms to keep the sheet around Aunt Sally as he moved toward me. With my end stretched tight and low, we rolled her into me. I braced her with my chest. Working together, with me taking most of her weight, we lowered her to the floor on the sheet.

Mr. Steinberg folded his section over her then kneeled and placed her hands on the gathered material. "Hold on, Sally!" he said.

He got to his feet, patted my shoulder, and said, "I'll clear the way."

Smoke covered the top part of the room, grew heavy, and dropped lower. I pulled up my mask, grabbed the ends of the sheet near Aunt Sally's toes and dragged her behind me.

Mr. Steinberg hurried ahead. Crouching under the

gray cloud, he kicked away bedpans, trays, and every other thing in our way. My back ached from stooping, pulling, and running without enough air. Dark smoke filled every space. I couldn't see.

Moving forward, I tried holding my breath, but coughed and coughed. Thought my lungs would give out. Felt a hand brush my leg.

"Here!" Mr. Steinberg sat in the stairwell, arms outstretched to catch and guide me. Only one flight down to the front door.

"Lift your head, Auntie!" My words felt like bits of coal. Smoke and heat turned them to tar on my tongue. Feared our insides would be glued and skin melted if we didn't move faster.

I hauled Aunt Sally so rough, she banged against each step, but told myself bruises weren't burns. We had to get out.

Mr. Steinberg spit up in the lobby but didn't stop. We made it out the front door, then slid down the stone steps to the sidewalk.

Heat smothered us and red embers swirled above. Aunt Sally moaned. No wagons or automobiles. No Su Ling, no one at all. The inferno roared, closing in on three sides.

I pointed to our only way out—the alley where the valet had parked the wagon. Knew it was gone now, but if we could reach that alley and get out the other side, we might escape the blaze.

Mr. Steinberg shook his head no. He put his palms on Aunt Sally's cheeks. With a weak smile on his lips, he drew Aunt Sally near. She nodded at him. None of us could speak. She touched my arm, then raised her thin hand and pointed a finger toward the alley, urging me to escape.

I pulled her sheet, but it wouldn't budge on the cement sidewalk.

Mr. Steinberg pushed me. "Go," he said breathlessly then mouthed the word again. He lowered his shaky frame over Aunt Sally to shield her from a shower of burning flakes.

"Please try," I begged, gasping for air through the mask. I took a step back then another.

Their faces touched in the tenderest way. They held each other. Flames clawed around the side of the hospital, stretched toward the entrance. Toward them.

My steps quickened. Put my hands on top of my head, turned, and ran.

When I got to the alley, I looked back. Screamed

for them to follow. Saw smoke and flames chasing me. Couldn't see them anymore.

Raced down the empty alley, reached the other side, and ran until the tip of my shoe caught the edge of something. My ankle snapped. I went down. Prayed the Lord would take me before the fire.

Chapter 20

Drums pounded. Echoing beats surged through me. An angel's voice beckoned from above.

"*Poverina!*"

A strange, familiar word. I blinked. Thought I'd see paradise. But it was the backside of a horse I glimpsed. Arms lifted me.

Mr. Caruso sat on the wagon's bench, holding the reins. His valet carried me around to the rear. Su Ling and the young woman pulled me in among the trunks.

The woman brushed hair from my face. "You're safe," she said.

Su Ling kissed my cheek.

"Hospital?" I asked, deep and throaty.

The wagon turned and we moved away from the raging fire, away from the hospital. The woman, Su Ling, and I clung to each other as we rocked and bounced.

My ankle slammed against the wagon bed. Pain seared through me then only a black nothing.

When I woke, my head rested in the lap of Su Ling's new friend. We were still in the back of the wagon, but it wasn't moving. Su Ling held the canteen of water to my lips. Her mask was around her neck, and so was mine.

I sipped and tried to sit up, but the young woman pressed my shoulder. "Rest," she said.

"Who are you?" I lifted my head to look at her face. Dizziness forced me to close my eyes, but I'd seen her kind smile.

"I'm Grace," she said. "A teacher at the Lutheran Mission School in Chinatown, until the fire destroyed it."

"Is, is the hospital gone too?" Didn't know how else to ask.

"I'm sorry, yes," she said.

I inhaled a big, clean breath of fresh air. Didn't smell smoke or taste ashes.

"Where are we?"

"The Presidio," Grace said. "Try to rest."

Had more questions, but my quivering chin and trembling lips kept me silent.

Su Ling put her small finger on my mouth. She said something in her language that sounded like *jaauh*.

"*Jie* means elder sister," Grace said. "Su Ling says you saved her life and have become her big sister."

"But...you...rescued...me." I sputtered out the words, because Su Ling's touch brought tears—heavy, splashing tears.

"Ah, *cara*, the pain is bad?" Mr. Caruso looked over the side of the wagon at my swollen ankle.

I shook my head. That kind of pain I could grit and bear, but how do you bear not being able to save your aunt and only friend? Hurt so much, I thought grief would swallow my heart. Could only pray God, in his mercy, would let them be a couple in eternity.

"They have room for you," Mr. Caruso said to me.

"In...Heaven?" I wiped my wet face on the sleeve of my nightgown. The white cotton had turned dark gray.

"Not yet, I think." He smiled at me.

The valet said, "It's time."

Lifting Su Ling out of the wagon, Mr. Caruso said, "I will miss you, *bambina*."

She nuzzled his neck.

He threw back his head and laughed a hardy, melodious laugh. Struck me hard. How could he be happy? But he was leaving. Leaving the burdens of this city, of me and Su Ling.

The valet helped Grace out of the wagon. Then he climbed up, gathered me in his arms, and eased himself and me to the ground. Holding on to him, I sniffled through my tears. "Thank you for coming back for me."

"*We* came back," Mr. Caruso said, still holding Su Ling. "All of us," he added.

Then he looked at his man. "Now we go to Oakland."

And to the rest of us he said, "You will be okay now."

The opera singer, his valet, Su Ling, and I had become a sort of family. We'd made it through the calamity together. I tightened my grip on the valet, didn't want to let go.

Mr. Caruso put Su Ling down next to Grace. "Take care of her."

He pulled a leather wallet from his pocket, removed some bills, and handed them to Grace. She tucked the money into her skirt pocket and shook his hand.

He walked over to me and bowed. "You, I will never forget. I wish you a good, long life, *cara*."

Weeping too much to speak, I lowered my head to

the most famous tenor in the world.

The valet carried me into a building and down a corridor filled with nurses, doctors, and soldiers, who moved among people like us, seeking help. So many people. He gently placed me on an empty bed.

A doctor came over. I recognized him. My hand flew to his face and knocked his glasses off.

The valet grabbed me, "No, no!"

"He's the one," I sobbed. "The one who took them."

The valet put himself in front of the doctor and said to me, "It was the fire. The fire. No one's fault."

The doctor looked surprised. He picked up his spectacles.

"Don't leave me," I said to the valet.

"Shush." He hugged me and didn't let go when the doctor removed my shoe. He held on when I cried out in pain. He whispered, "*Coraggio.*"

Sounded like courage. I didn't have any.

By the time the doctor had a splint on my ankle and wrapped it in bandages, the valet was gone. No goodbye. Didn't even know his name.

The doctor touched my nose. "Sore?"

I nodded.

"From the bruising, I'd say it's broken, but not

displaced or very swollen. Should heal in a few weeks."
He called a nurse over and told her to give me a sponge
bath and clean gown. He turned, started to walk away.

I found my voice. "I'm sorry."

He stopped. "All right," he said, coming back. "Why
did you hit me?" He sat on the bed and waited.

When I got to the part where he ran into Mr.
Steinberg with his automobile, a ruckus sounded down
the hall. Boots thumping. Squealing.

A man shouted, "Halt! Halt, I said!"

Su Ling's cries echoed.

"I'm here!" I yelled.

Su Ling and Grace, chased by a soldier, ran to my
bedside—all of them yammering at once.

The doctor motioned the soldier to follow him. They
walked a few paces away.

Out of breath, Grace said, "Thank goodness we
found you. They want to take us to another camp."

"No, they can't," I cried. "I need you. Tell them I
need you."

Chapter 21

Friday, April 20, 1906

After a good night's sleep in a real bed, I woke slowly with an empty head—for a few minutes at least. Didn't open my eyes, wasn't quite sure where I was, enjoyed drifting with no thoughts, until I yawned, stretched, and the pain brought everything back. Felt the thickness of the binding around my ankle. Saw a single crutch leaning against the bed.

Remembered the doctor told me yesterday there were too many broken bones in San Francisco, so only one crutch to a customer.

He recalled my aunt and Mr. Steinberg, but had no memory of me. Aunt Sally's injuries were so severe— internal bleeding, he said—that she might not have recovered from the fall out of her bedroom.

I suppose he thought hearing that news would somehow ease my grieving. It didn't.

But as I sat up, an idea began to form that might help. Wasted no time getting out of bed to learn how to walk with that crutch. Another patient, a few beds down, told me the trick was to take a small hop, balance, small hop, then try bracing my weight with the crutch to see if I could take a limp-step with the bad ankle.

Pain shot through me when I tried that. The hopping method worked, but soon wore me out. On my fifth lap down the hall, Grace and Su Ling met me.

"Brought you some clothes," Grace said. "Stood in the longest line for these. All they had that might fit you, I'm afraid." She handed me a pair of boy's breeches, a sweater, and socks.

I still had my own shoes. All that remained of what I'd brought to the city.

Chapter 22

Saturday, April 21, 1906

Grace, Su Ling, and I had our very own pup tent on the parade grounds. My hospital bed was needed by someone else, so the doctor arranged for the three of us to stay here until they could figure out how to get me back to my family. We slept on two layers of wool blankets with one more to cover us. Lying side by side in our tiny shelter kept us warm. But we all woke up hungry.

As Su Ling put on her tunic, I noticed the tag that had been tied around her neck was missing. I asked Grace about it.

"It had her grandfather's name and address on it," she said. "Su Ling and an older cousin had just arrived from China. They were waiting on the dock for their grandfather to meet them when the earthquake struck. Stacks of boxes and crates crashed around them and buried her cousin."

"Poor Su Ling." When I said her name, she looked over and smiled.

"How did she get to the stable?" I asked.

"She only remembers you. The child was terrified, probably ran until she couldn't anymore." Grace finger-combed Su Ling's black hair. "Her grandfather lived in Chinatown. But the fire destroyed everything there."

I decided to tell Grace my idea later. Last night I'd come up with a plan that I knew would be good for all three of us.

We made our way to the field kitchen and stood in line for breakfast. The Presidio was an Army post that had been turned into a refugee camp for thousands of people who'd lost their homes and possessions. There were lines everywhere. Lines of tents. Lines for food, clothes, blankets, and even for books. A painted sign on a wood plank had been propped up near the latrines: *Rooms for rent. Cheap. Furnish your own roof, walls, windows, and doors.*

San Franciscans didn't have much left except their sense of humor. And they sure didn't mind sharing what they had.

We found a spot on the grass to sit and eat. "Do you think Mr. Caruso managed to catch a train back east?" I asked Grace.

"Hope so."

"I was thinking about what these folks in the camp—including you, Su Ling, and I—lost in the earthquake and fires, and you know what's strange?"

She looked at me. "What?"

"That Mr. Caruso didn't lose one thing. He still had his great voice, his valet, and all his trunks and bags. Then he collected me, a wagon and horse, Su Ling, and you. When he left, he actually had more than he started with, three new friends!"

We laughed and it felt good. Even Su Ling giggled without knowing why, probably to keep us company.

A few men sitting nearby looked over at the noise we made. They moved away. Some women walking past stared and whispered.

Thought maybe the boy's clothes I had on bothered them, but when I heard one woman say, "Don't they know they don't belong here?" I understood. They didn't like having Grace and Su Ling close by.

Grace must have seen the anger in my eyes. She

hushed me before I said anything.

"You'll cause us trouble," she said.

"But it's so unfair. You've suffered from the earthquake just like them."

"There's a separate camp for the Chinese refugees," Grace said. "That's where the soldier wanted to take Su Ling and me, until your doctor said you needed to be with people you knew until you could be reunited with your family. But that could change if there are complaints."

At the mention of her name, Su Ling grinned and took a big bite of bread. She didn't seem aware of anything other than her meal and being safe with us.

"That's my plan!" I said. "You'll help me get to Paso Robles. And I know my family will reward you for it." But I didn't know that for sure. I reckoned they'd be so happy I'd made it home that they'd be kind to anyone who helped me. And wouldn't act like the foolish people here. Grandma might turn up her nose, but not Mama and Papa. And Joey was too young to be rude to anyone except me.

Chapter 23

Sunday, April 22, 1906

I tried to find the doctor after lunch to ask him if I could go to the Chinese camp with Grace and Su Ling. Angry looks from other refugees whenever we went to the latrines or stood in line for meals made me nervous. If Su Ling and Grace were taken to the other camp because people didn't want them here, I feared I'd never see them again. We couldn't be separated, no matter what. Su Ling was my sister. My plan was for her to live with me in Paso Robles. Grace said that wouldn't work, but I reckoned she didn't want to be left out.

I figured how Grace could stay too. Knew she'd be a much better teacher than Miss Hobson. I'd convince Papa to hire her as our tutor. She could teach Joey and me to speak Chinese while she taught Su Ling English. I'd thought it through but needed the doctor's help to keep us together. Couldn't find him anywhere inside the hospital.

Even though the hop-walking had me tuckered, I decided to look around the grounds one more time. Grace and Su Ling waited for me in our tent. Grace was anxious about the stares and whispers too.

I saw a man with a megaphone standing on top of an overturned box. He called for attention, asked everyone to gather around for an important announcement.

"Relief shipments from across the state and country are on their way," he said.

People clapped. I moved closer.

"Mayor Schmitz promises order will be maintained and our city will be rebuilt. But with so many of us homeless, an exodus is necessary to find lodging in undamaged towns. Helping in that cause, Mr. Harriman of the Southern Pacific Railroad has announced his trains will take refugees from San Francisco to other California destinations, free of charge."

The cheers were instant and loud. I remembered how Aunt Sally had complimented the efficiency of Mr. Harriman's railroad when my trunk was delivered to her apartment. Knew she'd appreciate his generosity. I cheered too.

The man told us where to sign up if we wanted to leave. I hobbled as fast as I could to our tent.

"Grace, tell Su Ling we're taking a train ride!"

Chapter 24

Monday, April 23, 1906

A caravan of five open wagons left the Presidio after breakfast. Grace, with Su Ling on her lap, and I were in the last transport, sitting with the driver. He was a young soldier who told us he was from Oregon and said he didn't mind being next to Chinese girls. We were happy not to be squished in the back of the wagon with the twenty refugees who did mind. They swayed like one person, even moaned at the same instant over each rut or bump.

As we snaked our way through San Francisco's smoldering ruins, the soldier said his state would ship tons of lumber for the rebuilding effort. Sooty dust, kicked up by the rigs ahead, had us coughing and using our hands to cover our noses and mouths.

I thought about the masks Mr. Caruso's valet had made. I tapped Su Ling, pretended to tie a hankie around my head. She held her hand flat across her nose, lifting it up and down, laughing.

"Glad you're so happy," the soldier said, looking at us. "But this reminds me of a funeral procession. And we're traversing the corpse."

Was going to tell him we were only remembering a game we played with friends we missed but kept it to myself. It was too hard to explain laughter in this devastated place.

At the train station, we thanked our soldier and wished him farewell. With so many folks leaving, I figured there'd never be another San Francisco like the one I stepped into last week from this very depot—no matter how much timber Oregon supplied. We joined our crowd of travelers, trudging off to stand in lines as long as the ones we waited in every day at the Presidio.

First, Grace checked the huge blackboard inside the station listing towns along the coastal route all the way to Los Angeles. Departure times were scrawled, erased, corrected—hard to read. Grace told me to stand in the telegraph line, insisting we had to tell my family to meet the southbound train, while she and Su Ling found the line to sign up for seats.

I endured an hour of inching ahead so slowly that my good foot ached as much as my broken ankle throbbed, and my underarm hurt from leaning so long on the crutch. I'd been with Aunt Sally when she sent the telegram letting my family know I'd arrived, but didn't know how to do it myself or what to say. As I neared the window, I saw that the man behind the counter had a deep crease in his brow from dealing with one anxious person after another.

Started me thinking it might be better to surprise Mama and Papa. Not have them fret if the train was late or wonder who I was or wasn't bringing home with me. Before I could step out of line, Grace and Su Ling were at my side.

Grace panted. "We had to run. So many people in our line. But it's all right. Train leaves in forty-five minutes."

When the telegraph agent saw Grace, he said, "We don't send no Chinese messages."

She stared at him.

"Understand English, missy?"

"She's a teacher," I said.

Grace nudged me aside.

"Speaks better than you," I muttered under my breath. I couldn't abide the way she and Su Ling were treated by people who didn't want them around because they looked different. If they knew Su Ling and Grace like I did, they would be ashamed of themselves.

"It's not for me, sir," Grace said. "We need to tell this child's family she's alive and will be delivered to them tonight."

He shoved a paper and pencil toward Grace. "No more 'an ten words, missy."

I tilted my head in front of the window. "The Golden Rule is my favorite. What's yours?"

He ignored me. Grace neatly printed the message and returned the paper. The agent read it back. "Morgan Family (stop) Paso Robles (stop) Meet SF train tonight (stop)."

She nodded her approval.

"Four bits," he said.

She hesitated.

I worried she didn't have fifty cents but remembered Mr. Caruso had given her money.

"Trains might be free, but the telegraph ain't." He squinted at her. "Understand?"

Grace put two quarters on the counter.

The man shooed us away. Shouldn't have sassed him, but he was in the wrong and I couldn't hold it in. Turned around to see the agent hunched over to help an old woman write something. They looked like wilted flowers. Felt bad for being rude. But why didn't grown-ups follow the same Sunday school lessons they teach children?

Grace double-checked the train schedule on the smudged blackboard. People brushed against us, hurrying here and there. Policemen and railroad workers shouted above the noise of all the footsteps and voices. Whistles blew. I wobbled for balance and searched the board for my hometown's name to feel the comfort of familiar letters.

The last time I was in this station, Aunt Sally was fluttering her lace-trimmed handkerchief at my train. I'd vowed she'd never change me. Then the wondrous city had cast its magic spell. And Mr. Steinberg took us to the opera. Less than a week ago.

Closed my eyes to stop the memories, but I saw my auntie waving at me, and I swear she had a smile under her turned-up nose. Was it there that day I arrived? Had I dreamed it just now?

Grace shouted in my ear, "We have to get to the train!" Shepherding us to a long line on the outside platform, she said, "You'll get hungry. I saved this bread for you." She put something wrapped in paper into my hand. The little parcel was warm from being inside her skirt pocket. Made me think of the buttermilk biscuits Grandma had given me.

"Hope they have seats for all of us," I said, trying to clear the past from my mind.

A conductor held a clipboard as he made his way down the line, checking names off a list. Grace said something, but the man's voice boomed over her. He told people in front of us to be patient and not ask so many questions. "We're doing the best we can under the circumstances," he said.

Wondered if Su Ling and Grace were nervous about going to Paso Robles. "Tell Su Ling my brother, Joey, is younger than her." I remembered the Chinese word Grace had taught me for *elder sister*. "She can be a *jie*, like me." Leaning on my crutch, I smiled at Su Ling, waited for Grace to translate.

She didn't say anything.

"Did you hear me?" I asked.

Grace touched my arm. "We can't go with you."

"Of course you can. You put your names down, didn't you?"

"Only yours."

"Won't they let you on the train? I'll raise a stink."

"No!" Grace held me back. "Su Ling and I belong here with our own kind."

"But I'm your kind and you're mine. She's my little sister, you're my friend." I took a deep breath. "You're more my kind than anyone. We...we belong together now. You have to come with me."

"It wouldn't be good for us or for you. I told you this last night. It wouldn't be fair to your family."

"But you have to help me get home. You told the doctor—you promised me. My folks will take care of you." Even I heard the doubt in my voice.

"We're here with you to see you off, to make sure you get home safely," Grace said. "You'll be with your family tonight."

"You can't have Su Ling," I said. "We're sisters. We saved each other!"

Su Ling began to tremble. My tone scared her. Felt bad about that, but I couldn't lose one more person I cared about.

Grace looked straight into my eyes. "We're staying here. Su Ling is not yours to have."

"What's the trouble?" The conductor towered over us.

"It's a hard good-bye, sir. We're all right," Grace said.

"Are you sure?" he asked me.

I nodded, blinking back tears.

The conductor moved down the line.

"My work is here," Grace said. "The mission will rebuild the school, and I want to establish an orphanage with it."

"Then let Su Ling come with me." I tried once more. "She's important to me." I rubbed the sweater sleeve under my nose.

Grace said something to Su Ling, and she said something back. Couldn't understand them.

Holding my arm out to Su Ling, I said, "*Mei*, come with me." Grace had told me that meant little sister. *Jie* and *mei* were the only words I knew in their language.

Su Ling hugged me, but quickly drew back, shook her head, and held on to Grace's hand.

She wanted Grace, not me. Thought my heart would stop beating. I'd found her, comforted her, laughed with her. But it was Grace she ran to at the Railroad Hospital. Talking and talking in strange words I didn't know.

"If Su Ling's grandfather is alive," Grace said, "he'll be among our people. Probably at the Chinese camp.

I'll take care of her, I promise."

How could I have forgotten? I'd asked Mr. Caruso if we could find Su Ling's people after we found mine. But when Aunt Sally and Mr. Steinberg...I bit my lip. "I'll stay. Help you look for him."

Grace stared at me then said, "You can't."

Could barely breathe—the sting of her words a painful shock, almost like a slap.

I knew what she meant. I couldn't help, couldn't speak their language, and couldn't keep Su Ling from trying to find her grandfather.

The conductor yelled, "All aboard!"

Deep inside, I understood there was something else I couldn't do. Bring back the people I'd lost by holding on to Su Ling and Grace.

They stayed next to me, moving forward with the line.

"We are your friends," Grace said. "Always your friends."

The conductor gripped my arm to help boost me up the steps. I dragged the crutch like an anchor pulled from its mooring.

Chapter 25

Took a seat by the window. It felt too much like before. Being sent away. Alone. This time my heart wouldn't let me turn away. I pressed my face and hands against the glass. They were standing right there, waving, crying too. "Please write!" I shouted.

Grace nodded, lifting Su Ling so she could see me better. I blew kisses. So did they. The train chugged out of what was left of San Francisco.

I studied the wrapped piece of bread still in my hand. A woman toting a chubby baby boy sank into the seat next to me. I offered the food to her.

Must have fallen asleep against the mother, because I woke with a start when that baby of hers kicked me in the head.

"Sorry. You okay?"

I rubbed my temple.

"You've been asleep for hours," she said. "Almost asked the conductor to check on you."

"Are we near Paso Robles?"

"We've been delayed several times for relief freight heading north. Haven't reached Salinas yet." She smiled at her child. "We're going to Santa Barbara. My husband's family lives there."

Her son fussed and fidgeted. She cooed.

I looked out at the darkness but saw only a reflection of the inside of the compartment in the soft lamplight. All seats filled by a ragtag collection of passengers with mismatched clothes, slouched shoulders, and tired faces. Some folks dozed, some chatted.

The mother sang to her babe, gently swaying back and forth. Her sweet tune brought back Mama's lullabies for Joey. Made me ache for long, long ago when Mama rocked me too.

Mr. Steinberg had laughed when I told him my name was Littlebeth. He said I'd outgrown it. Now I yearned for it to fit again.

Knew my family would be relieved I'd made it out of

the inferno—hoped that would help them tolerate having me home again. The mother brushed against me as she moved with her boy. Thought about Joey. Wanted to feel his sticky smooches and hear him giggle.

Closed my eyes, pictured our house, remembered the good smells in Mama's kitchen. I'd ask her to teach me to cook. Didn't want to grow up not knowing how—only eating sardines and crackers like Aunt Sally.

What kind of lady would she have turned me into? My auntie wasn't the silent, sweet, soft kind Grandma wanted me to be. Aunt Sally had to be strong and smart to run her own business and live alone. I'd seen her stubborn side too when she was rejecting Mr. Steinberg. Until the end. A thought shoved its way in. What if Papa and Grandma blamed me for not saving their Sally? If their hearts were too broken to want me back?

"Not easy, is it?" the mother said, patting her baby's back. His head lolled against her chest. Drool streamed from his lips, down the round knob of his chin, onto his mother's blouse.

I stared, not sure if she was talking to me or her son. His slobber would soak her to the bone soon. Pulling a hankie from under the cuff of her sleeve, she reached over to stroke my cheek and wipe under my nose. The flowing mess on my face startled me as much as her touch.

"Does your ankle hurt?" She handed me the cloth—plain cotton, not at all like the fancy handkerchiefs Aunt Sally sold.

"No." I clutched the hankie until it became a damp wad inside my fist. "I have to tell my family something bad, and I don't know how."

The woman kissed the top of her baby's head. "Uh-huh." She looked at me with the weariest eyes. "Not easy for any of us."

She began to hum to her son again. I realized everyone in this carriage, all of us on this train, had been through something no one who hadn't experienced it would ever understand. We'd survived a terrible catastrophe, yet we were all grieving.

"Ma'am?" A girl about my age stood in the aisle, her hand on the mother's shoulder. "Would you change seats with me? My mama wants to share some bread and apple jelly with you and your baby."

The woman and I looked up at the girl.

"Not enough for you," she said to me then took a step back to let the mother and child out.

"Hello," I said when the girl sat down.

"I don't like to talk to people I don't know," she said.

"Can't make new friends that way." I thought about how hard it was to make friends even when you talked a lot.

"I like the ones I already have." She had a prissy tone and prickly expression.

"Where are they?" I asked.

She didn't say anything, but I saw the answer in her eyes. She'd left them behind when she got on this train.

Decided I'd tell her about myself so she'd know who I was then she could decide if she wanted to talk to me.

After a while, she gave in and told me her name was Abigail. She and her mother were going to stay with a cousin in Paso Robles while her father salvaged his printing business and rebuilt their house in San Francisco.

The conductor came through announcing our town. I took a deep breath. He saw my crutch. "Let me help you."

"Good luck," my new friend said.

"You too." I took the conductor's arm and hoped I'd find the right words for my family.

Chapter 26

Tuesday, April 24, 1906

It was past midnight when we pulled into Paso Robles, yet even in the dark I could tell nothing had changed. Buildings stood firm. Was relieved there were no piles of bricks or ruptured pipes or burned ruins on our streets.

Lantern lights flickered around the edges of the depot's platform. A few people waited to greet folks who got off the train. They shared quick embraces, quiet exchanges. Abigail waved good-bye when she and her mother left with their cousin.

No one was waiting for me.

The conductor stayed by my side. He checked his pocket watch. "Family meeting you?"

"Maybe they didn't get the telegram," I said. Hoped

that's all it was. That I'd be welcomed—or at least *allowed*—back. "My house isn't far. I can walk."

He eyed my crutch. "What's your name?"

Before I could answer, Mama and Papa called out as they ran across the platform.

I hopped toward them, my nose running, tears welling.

"Littlebeth!" Mama rushed for me. Papa passed her and lifted me in a bear hug. My crutch fell.

The conductor handed it to me then climbed the steps of the train car and signaled the engineer. He didn't call: *All aboard.* There weren't any refugees leaving our town.

"So sorry we weren't here," Mama said. "We *were* here before then we had to leave and we…My goodness, did someone hit you?" She stared at my face.

Papa talked over her, just as fast. "Joey and Mother were with us but got tired so we took them back to the house, and I realized we'd need the wagon. Had a terrible time hitching the horses. Too excited, I think. Where's Sally? And your trunks?"

Mama touched my crutch, looked down at my bandaged ankle. "We've been so worried, Littlebeth." She spoke slower, a quaver in each word.

"I'm all right, Mama. But call me Beth now."

Papa set me down and kissed my forehead. "Suits you." He started to say something else then pressed his lips together. Without waiting for an answer to the question about his sister, we walked to the wagon. Oh, I wish Mr. Steinberg could have met my papa.

Grandma and Joey were on the sofa in our parlor when I hobbled into the house. She had my brother nestled in her arms. "Did his best, but he couldn't stay awake."

She watched as I made my way to her but didn't say anything about the crutch or the boy's breeches I had on.

I sat next to them, felt the warmth of both as I leaned against Grandma's side. We waited for Mama and Papa to come in and settle into their chairs. Then it was time.

"Aunt Sally was a brave lady."

* * *

My bruises soon faded. Within two months my ankle healed, but I'll never run as fast as I used to. Papa says that's a good thing for the boys in town.

Hearts don't mend as fast. Still hurts whenever I think of my auntie and Mr. Steinberg. Grandma says she'll wear black the rest of her days, but I believe it's a comfort knowing her daughter loved a good man who cherished her—that they held each other close during their final moments.

My spirits rose considerably when the letter from Mr. Caruso arrived with his sketches of Su Ling and me. He addressed it to Signorina Morgan, General Delivery, Paso Robles, California. Mailed it from New York City before he returned to Italy. He even included a drawing of Bully-Boy Teddy for Papa! That same day Grandma baked an apple pie just for me.

I've given speeches about the Great Quake to every school, church, and club in town to raise money for the San Francisco Relief Fund and for the Chinese Lutheran Mission School and Orphanage.

Grace and Su Ling write a letter every week. Well, Grace writes. Su Ling prints her name under the pictures she draws. They haven't found her grandfather yet.

I'm doing extra chores to earn enough for train tickets so they can visit me. Mama and Papa want to meet them.

Been too busy for any cowgirl escapades. But I did promise Abigail that before she moves back to San Francisco, I'll show her where some famous outlaws once laid low.

Discussion Questions

1. What can you infer about society in 1906 from the book?

2. What are Littlebeth's first impressions of Aunt Sally? Why does she feel the way she does?

3. How does Mr. Steinberg treat Littlebeth when he finds her looking for the fish market?

4. Littlebeth experiences a strange churning in her stomach in chapter 7. What is the cause? What does she decide to do about it? Have you had to cope with that feeling?

5. After the shock of the earthquake, Littlebeth helps Mr. Steinberg and Aunt Sally. What problem-solving skills does she use?

6. Littlebeth believes her family sent her away to be free of her. What decision does she make that shows she wants to act differently than her family?

7. Even though Littlebeth is grateful for Mr. Caruso's help, she notices something about his attitude that bothers her when they are at the first hospital and again at the second hospital. What is it, and why do you think it troubles her?

8. At the Presidio Army Camp, Littlebeth thinks, "The opera singer, his valet, Su Ling, and I had become a sort of family." Why does she feel that way?

9. What affected you most about the farewell scene with Mr. Caruso?

10. While Littlebeth, Grace, and Su Ling are eating their breakfast at the refugee camp, a group of women stare and whisper about them. Why? How does Littlebeth react? How does Grace respond?

11. At the train station, Littlebeth says to Grace and Su Ling, "You're more my kind than anyone." What does she mean by that?

12. Why doesn't Su Ling want to go to Paso Robles with Littlebeth? How does Littlebeth react?

13. Why do you think it is easier for Littlebeth to make a new friend on the train ride home?

14. How does Littlebeth change from the beginning of the book to the end? Give examples.

15. Which of Littlebeth's character traits do you wish you had? Why?

Acknowledgments

When I moved to Paso Robles, Juddi Morris asked me to join a group of people interested in writing. That's how it started. I wrote a short story about a headstrong girl who lived here a long time ago. Juddi said it needed to be a book.

I was already spending a lot of time at the Carnegie Library researching our town's past for newspaper articles so I thought it would be fun to write a historical novel. Many years and rewrites later, I actually did it, but not alone.

The Cambria Writers Workshop, whose talented, generous members began this journey with me, kept the story on track. I'm forever grateful to them.

The Kiddie Writers invited me to participate as my manuscript progressed. They made sure I reached the final chapter. The expert critique of Juddi Morris, Sherry Shahan, Sharon Lovejoy, Elizabeth Spurr, Elizabeth Van Steenwyk, Lori Peelen, Helen K. Davie, Cynthia Bates, Veronica DeCoster, Stephanie Roth Sisson, and Natalie Jarboe was invaluable.

Sherry Shahan believed in me even when I was uncertain. She insisted my manuscript was ready to submit, and knew where it would be a good fit. There aren't enough letters in *thank you* for all she's done.

Andrea Hall, a terrific editor, saw something she liked in my character Littlebeth. She deepened and strengthened the story by asking the right questions. I'm so lucky to have such a perceptive partner.

Albert Whitman and Company, publishers of the Boxcar Children series—the first books that kept me up, reading under the covers with a flashlight when I was little—made a dream come true. I'm proud to be a Whitman author.

Kyle Letendre, the artist who created the book jacket illustration, captured a haunting image of discovery. It's a thrill to have his work represent my book.

I appreciate the guidance and encouragement of

Catherine Ryan Hyde, Vicki Leon, Jeff Prostovich, Olga Essex and Madeleine Gallagher beyond measure.

Family puts my life and writing into context and gives it meaning. With my husband, Curt, everything is possible. Our son, Jess, and daughter, Kate, continue to inspire, delight, and open the world.

Curtis Rankin

Cindy Rankin lived in five states and three European countries before finding a hometown in Paso Robles, California. Her love of this area, its history and people, sparked her imagination. She joined local writing groups and began creating characters and stories for fun. Cindy also raised a son and daughter here while working as a freelance writer and substitute teacher. She and her husband continue to live in Paso Robles.